48 Hours in Heaven

Author: John M. Duhnovsky

48 Hours in Heaven
Copyright © 2017

ISBN: 9781794171718

Table of Contents

Introduction

I would like to start by saying that heaven is a place where love is pure and true. Like a virgin forest is untouched by man, heaven is a place untouched by sin. God's very identity is love, and heaven is a place that He invited us to live so we can experience His love for ourselves. It's an unbelievable eternal life of discovering the depth of His love for us.

This novel will give you a glimpse of what heaven could be like if you choose to accept His invitation. It's fast-paced as you enter into one amazing event after another. In this novel the characters drive their car to heaven, which we know can't be done, but other than that I think you will find it to be very biblically accurate. In order to help you get the best understanding of this topic, I am asking that you think of heaven as a town. We'll simply call it Godville. At the end of this story I come back and share some very valuable insights. This novel was written by the inspiration of the Holy Spirit, for the purpose of revealing to all people the love God has for them.

Now I would like to introduce to you the two main characters, Bill and Sue Thompson. They got married in their mid-twenties after meeting in college. They loved to dream about what their lives were going to look like. They often talked about their friends and how their marriages were not doing well. They believed it was caused by a lack of planning. Bill and Sue were the organized types, and they decided to sit down and plan out their whole lives together. During the first year of marriage they worked hard to come up with the perfect plan. It was a miracle that their marriage survived this as they began to discover how different they really were.

When they completed their plan they were so proud of the accomplishment, and they were confident that this would all but guarantee them picture perfect lives, a picture perfect family, in a picture perfect world. Life was great! They had a big celebration for what they had accomplished, believing it would set them up for their future success. Now our story begins.

Chapter 1

WE STILL HAVE EACH OTHER

Thirty-eight years later, Bill took Sue to a nice restaurant to celebrate their anniversary. Bill started the conversation by looking back in time. He said, " Sue, it's hard to believe what we have been through these last thirty eight years. How many times did you and I try so very hard to stick with our plan?"

Sue said, " Yeah, I remember thinking to myself how out of control our lives were. I often asked myself, *what in the world is going on?* I could never really find the answer. There is one thing I have discovered, though. I do know that you're a good man. You have proven that to me over the years. You always loved me and the kids. It's just so hard to believe things turned out the way they did."

Bill responded, "Yes, it is, honey, but for some reason this world has the ability to change people's lives even when they have done all they could to make the right decisions."

"Well, Sue, I know the only thing we really have left that was in our plans, are you and me. I got you and you got me."

Sue said," Yeah, for better or for worse, right?"

He looked at her and said," Yes honey for better or for worse." Bill continued saying, " We have proven our faithfulness to each other."

She agreed and said, " Because of this I trust you and I will follow you wherever you take me."

Bill thought to himself, *what an honor that is, for her to believe in me that much.* He knew their hope wasn't crushed. He knew there were enough pieces to use to rebuild their lives and get on the right road this time. Bill felt the pain of disappointment and he saw it in Sue as well. Bill said, " Sue, I love you so much and I know how hard life has been for you. I just want the rest of our lives to be peaceful and pleasant, no more stress, disappointments or unexpected disasters."

Bill began sharing some of the deepest desires he had for her. He said," Sue, if I was able to make one wish, it would be to take you to a place where you would never again experience the pains and agonies that this life has brought you. I don't quite understand this, but I must tell you that I love you so much more than I have been able to show you. All I know is I loved you the best I knew how."

Sue was touched by this and said, "Yes, dear, I know you did. There were just so many distractions, so many things that seemed so urgent. I can look back and see all the things that continually put our love and affection for each other farther down the to do list. Even when it did become a priority, we were still so consumed by the issues of the day that we couldn't just stop and enjoy each other. I remember how many times on vacations we had to stop each other from discussing these issues. Why couldn't we just stop! It was as if someone else was controlling our thoughts."

She continued saying," You probably remember the time we went to South Haven for the weekend. It was just before the kids' accident."

He said," Yes I do."

"Well, Bill, I can't tell you how much I was looking forward to that getaway. Now, honey, you surely know by now that when I am thinking about a getaway, especially a romantic place like South Haven, I have got it all planned out. You know what I'm saying, dear?"

He grinned and said, " Yes, I do, and I hope you have been planning for tonight as well." She just looked at him and smiled.

Bill said," If I'm thinking right, that trip was two months after I started our business and I purchased our first truck. Oh yeah, do you remember Clementine?"

Sue responded with a short, disgusted laugh, "You really made me mad!" I remember thinking, 'He's got a lot of gall, telling me how much he loves someone else.' You know you really blew it, right?"

Bill just responded by shaking his head in agreement.

Sue said, "All the romance was gone and I was left with a multitude of emotions that were just the opposite of romance. I demanded to know who she was, and you

9

giggled then told me it's not a personal thing and I shouldn't take it that way. I got even madder if that's possible. Then you added more fuel to the fire by telling me to settle down. You're lucky there wasn't a gun in our room. Then finally after you had taken things to the limit you decide to stop playing your little game. I was really upset as you just sat on the edge of the bed, smiling as if you knew something I didn't. I remember at that point that you were not serious, so I settled down a little. If I recall I sarcastically said, 'Okay, Mr. Comedian, tell me the rest of the story."

Bill remembered that he had giggled as he told her that Clementine wasn't a girl, it was his new truck.

Sue responded," I should have known, guys name everything they value. You wouldn't get away with that trick today. I know you too well."

Bill said, "Yeah, you're probably right. I think we need to look at what we are talking about right now. Hey, it's our anniversary. Let's focus on something other than the stupid things we did years ago."

Bill and Sue laughed together and enjoyed each other for the rest of the evening.

CHAPTER 2

BILL'S SEARCH FOR PARADISE

I spent the next month or so thinking about Sue. I watched her while she went about living her life. She was like a busy little beaver making sure everything around the house was taken care of. I noticed that my love for her was growing. I began to see more and more that all the things she was doing was to demonstrate her love and respect for me. I was more determined than ever to find a place for us to live where we could focus on our love and relationship, which are the things we had come to value the most. I longed to find this place for her. I wasn't sure if what we were looking for even existed. *Well, I thought, I'll never know unless I try.*

I told Sue that I was actively searching for the perfect place for us to live. I checked everywhere. I racked my brain. I must have spoken to fifty realtors, all claiming to have the perfect place for us. After visiting twenty-two paradise properties in four different countries, we became discouraged, realizing the best we could do was to live in a prettier house in a prettier place. That was not what we were looking for. I had serious doubts whether this kind of place even existed. I didn't tell Sue, but I had given up trying.

One day I received a phone call from a person who said he had found just what we were looking for. I asked him who he was and how he got my name. He said," I'm a representative of Godsville and I was given your name by two close friends of yours."

I sarcastically asked him, "And who might these close friends of mine be?"

He just giggled and said, " I was told to keep it a surprise and their identity would be revealed later."

Bill said, "Are you telling me that I should believe you? I don't even know you. How am I supposed to trust you?"

He replied," I'm not asking that you trust me because I'm just the messenger. What I am asking is if you can put your trust in your two closest friends who sent me."

Again I asked, "And who might these close friends be?"

There was just silence on the phone. I noticed a real battle going on inside of me. First, I was thinking, *This guy is nuts. How could he expect me to believe anything he says.* It certainly would be reasonable to be suspicious; after all, there are a lot of crazies out there.

I wanted to just blow this guy off, but something inside me told me to trust him and go. Then I thought about how burned out I was from trying to find that perfect place for Sue. I did notice that this guy was different from the rest. He didn't give me some hyped up sales pitch; he just invited me to check it out. I could have given him a thousand reasons not to go, but whether it was my curiosity of who these close friends were or my deep desire to find this place for Sue, I'm not sure.

Before I had actually made my decision I heard myself tell him," Yes, we will go." I couldn't believe I had just said that. WOW, that was weird! Oh, well, everything about this situation was weird. So we decided to meet in Godsville on Wednesday at nine in the morning. He gave me the directions, thanked me, and hung up. I started to walk to the kitchen to tell Sue when I suddenly stopped. I realized how crazy this whole thing was. I had never heard of this place, I didn't know who I talked to, I didn't know who my friends were, and to be perfectly honest I didn't understand the directions and he never gave me an address. How could I even try to get her to understand this when I didn't even understand it myself?

I thought, *Well maybe I can research this more and try to figure it out.* So I did my homework and wrote everything down. Then I examined all the notes and realized it made me even more confused. I just wanted her to have some hope. I said to myself, *Why does this have to be so difficult? Why can't I just go in there and tell her?*

Then I answered myself, *because this whole thing doesn't make sense? I don't even have good directions.* I knew I had to at least try, but I just couldn't see myself explaining it face to face. I knew she would ask a bunch of questions and I couldn't answer any of them. All I knew was something inside of me said to go. So finally I decided the best way to tell her was to write her a letter and make sure I wasn't home when she got it. I went to my office to write the letter. After rewriting it at least ten times in an attempt to make sense of it, I just gave up and wrote what little information I had and decided that had to be good enough.

I started to read....

> *Sue, have I got good news for you!*
> *Today I received a phone call from*
> *someone I don't know, and whose*
> *name I never got. He said that two*
> *very close friends of ours had asked*
> *him to call us to let us know that*
> *they have found the place we have*
> *been looking for. Of course I asked*
> *him who these close friends were,*
> *but he would only say they would*
> *reveal their identity to us later. I*
> *really challenged this guy, honey. I*
> *told him, "Are you asking me to trust*
> *what you're saying? I don't even*

know you." All he would say was he's just giving me a message from our two closest friends. What else could I say to him? After all, we can trust our closest friends, can't we?

Now, honey, I've never heard of this town before and to be honest, I'm not even sure where it is. This guy that I don't know gave me the directions and said it was easy because there was only one way to get there. We are to meet whoever this guy is in Godsville. We meet him Wednesday at nine in the morning. Please don't ask any questions.

Signed,

Your loving husband in whom you said you could trust.

I folded it up, put it in an envelope, and addressed it to her with no return address. I looked at my watch and realized that I needed to get to the post office before they closed. I hurried over there and arrived just as they were closing. I went to the window, fortunately the postman was my neighbor, Ted. He asked me why I looked so nervous, I told him it was because I was in a rush to get here before he closed. Ted said, " Yep, that was a close one, but you made it." Little did he know why I was really nervous. I knew I couldn't explain it to him either. I asked him when this letter would arrive.

Ted thought for a moment, "Well, today is Thursday....I'd say tomorrow at two in the afternoon."

"Okay, " I replied, as I paid him for the stamp.

As I was leaving Ted yelled, "Wait a minute, Bill."

I stopped as he said, "Do you know this is addressed to your house?"

I said, "I'm aware of that."

I could tell Ted was curious and wanted to talk to me more about that. I didn't give him a chance; I just left and went back home.

Now, I thought, *I just have to figure out an excuse to leave the house tomorrow afternoon.* This whole thing began to really bother me. I couldn't wrap my brain around it. I felt like I needed to talk to some people and get their opinions, but I knew I would just look like I was crazy. I figured trying to get people to understand something that I didn't understand myself would do nothing more than get me thrown in the nut house.

That night when we went to bed, Sue noticed I was having a hard time falling asleep. She said, "Bill, I noticed you were trying to avoid me this evening and now I see you can't seem to fall asleep. Is there anything wrong? You know I'm here to listen."

I just laid there looking at the ceiling, I didn't know how to respond to her.   Why does she always know when there is something bothering me? Finally, I just told her, "I will talk to you tomorrow, but don't worry because it is good news."

Her response to me wasn't helpful at all. She said, "Well, okay, I will wait until tomorrow, but you are acting very weird for someone who has good news."

I told her," I agree," and then under my breath I said, "Yeah, everything about this is weird." I was really happy she left it at that. I lay there for another two hours before falling asleep.

That night I had a dream I had told Ted (you know the postman and a part time barber) my story. So as soon as the post office closed, Ted went to his part time job (Need I say more?). Of course, the word got out all over town, and the next thing I knew I was being picked up by those guys in the white coats. They threw me in the back of a pickup truck (you know how dreams are) and took me to this crazy place. The next thing I knew, I was being interviewed by a person who was wacky enough to be sitting on my side of the desk. I couldn't take it anymore so I decided to leave my dream.

I woke up in a sweat just as my wife was returning to bed after a bathroom visit. Great timing! She saw that I was all sweaty and said," Honey, are you feeling alright? It looks like you have a fever." As she was speaking, she returned to the bathroom to get the thermometer so she could check my temperature. I didn't say anything, I just let her check it and, of   course, it was normal.

She patted me on the head and said, "Now you go back to sleep, dear. Everything will be fine." I just agreed and smiled at her. I knew I wasn't fooling her. I thought to myself, as I stared at the ceiling, *I don't want to go to sleep it's not worth the risk of another dream.* Of course, I did eventually fall asleep, and I slept well for the remaining two hours.

The next morning Sue was up bright and early. I could smell the bacon cooking and the coffee brewing. I really wanted to get out of bed and enjoy some coffee and breakfast but I still hadn't figured out the story I had to tell her so I wouldn't be home when the letter came. This would be quite difficult because I forgot today was "honey do list" day. I didn't know what to do, but I could hear the coffee and breakfast calling me.

So I got up to eat and tried to block out my problem and enjoy our breakfast. I could see that Sue was excited about me tackling the "honey do" list. I just acted like I was happy, too. We discussed the list for a while and planned out a couple of the projects. I could see she liked that but little did she know I just wanted to keep my mind off the letter.

I tackled the projects, but In the back of my mind I knew I had to be out of the house by one o'clock to be safe. I still wasn't sure how I was going to handle it. At 12:30, Sue came into the bedroom where I was hanging some pictures for her. She said, "That really looks nice honey, you do good work."

I just smiled and said," Yeah, honey, I just got the touch."

She said, "Lunch is ready, so wash up and meet me in the kitchen."

Then she unknowingly dropped the bomb when she said, "I noticed the mailman delivered early today, so while you wash up I'll get the mail."

I was thinking, *I don't believe it! They never come early! It's like the weirdness never ends.* So I washed up and sat down in the kitchen just as she walked in. She had prepared a very good lunch, and I let her know that I appreciated it. She thanked me as she was thumbing through the mail.

I just started to eat when I hear her say, "Well, this is interesting - a letter for me, but there's no return address. I wonder who that could be." Her curiosity was high enough that she immediately opened it, took the letter out, and began to read it to herself.

Boy, was I nervous! I didn't want to get into this now, but I guess I had no choice. I waited quietly as she continued reading. I was watching her facial expressions to see if I could figure out what her reaction would be. When she was done, she put the letter back in the envelope and she started to eat her lunch. I could see she was processing it.

Suddenly she started to shout in celebration. I was shocked, I didn't expect this type of reaction at all. She looked at me with a big smile on her face and said." I bet you were having a hard time holding back this good news." I was totally caught off guard. She never asked me a question, she just said, "I can't wait until we leave."

I just thought, *The weirdness just goes on and on.*

Chapter 3

NEVER IN MY WILDEST DREAMS

Several days passed, and Sue never asked me any questions. All she talked about was how excited she was to go. Again I thought, another weirdness. The day had come for us to leave for Godsville, and Sue was so excited. She asked, "Honey, do you think we should pack for an overnight stay?"

I told her I had not planned for this to be an overnight stay so we didn't need to bring anything extra. So we got in the car and took off down the road. Sue was so excited, I didn't recall ever seeing her this excited before. I wasn't sure why. She must have known something I didn't. I was so focused on her that I had no idea where I was going. I never even thought about the directions at all. All I could say is I was driving. The next thing I saw was Sue pointing her finger towards a billboard and yelling, "That's it! That's where we are going!"

As we got closer, I saw a beautiful gold-ish reflection coming from what appeared to be Main Street. As we entered the edge of town, the road was blocked by a dozen or more people all celebrating our arrival. I stopped the car, and they ran up to us, opened the doors, and helped us out. We just stood there looking at each other as I thought, *"Can these people be real?"* We had never felt such love and acceptance.

They placed a robe of royalty on each of us and guided us to a beautiful horse drawn carriage. They assisted us as we got in. Once we sat down, I leaned over to Sue and whispered , "I wonder how much this is going to cost?" It was as if they were celebrating our arrival.

With each step the horse took I experienced a deeper level of royalty coming upon me. It was as if we were the ones to be honored. Sue was so moved that tears began rolling down her cheeks. On the seat next to me I saw a beautiful silk cloth. I reached down and handed it to her so she could wipe her tears. I realized someone had already put it there for her, as if they knew she would need it.

Then Sue looked at me and our eyes connected.

I thought, *I somehow see him in a different way. He was a man worthy of honor and respect.* He softly said to me, "I love you." It was amazing, I had never before felt such a love come from him. It was as if his whole being had changed. His words, I love you, reached so far in me that I felt it connect to my heart.

As we traveled further into the town, we were amazed by the buildings, and the people. Everything was full of life. All the building looked new. They sparkled as the sun reflected off the precious metals and stones that were used to beautify the buildings. Everything in the town was fresh - as if it was cleaned just before our arrival.

I noticed that the street was golden in color; as I looked closer I realized they were streets of gold. I was shocked. All I could do was to nudge Bill and point down towards the street. Every step the horses took revealed more of the beauty of this town and its people. There was no poverty anywhere. I noticed that the cheers of celebration behind us were becoming louder.

When I looked back I was shocked by what I saw. I said," Bill look behind us."

He was amazed. What we saw were thousands of people celebrating our arrival. I realized that every person we had passed in the buggy had ran behind us shouting in celebration. My husband, who never had been much for showing emotion, was openly crying. It was an overwhelming experience.

A few short blocks later, we began to travel uphill to what appeared to be a magnificent mansion that was built on top of a hill in the center of town. My husband asked the carriage driver, "What is that mansion looking place on top of the hill?"

He replied, "That's where I'm taking you."

I looked at my wife and asked, "Sue, do you think that's the town manager's house? "

The carriage driver overheard me. He laughed and said, "That's where the king of Godsville and his son live. I am taking you there. You are their guests of honor."

My wife whispered to me, "What did we do to deserve this?"

I responded by shrugging my shoulders.

As we traveled higher and higher up the hill, the presence of love became stronger and stronger to the point where my wife and I were paralyzed in our seats. We couldn't do anything but receive this love inside us. Finally, our carriage stopped on the circle drive in front of the mansion. We were still frozen in our seats.

Then suddenly we felt a warmth inside us . This warmth was filled with love and acceptance. As it continued to consume me, I noticed that all nervousness was gone. In fact, I felt very comfortable and at peace. I felt like I was going to meet for the first time someone I longed to meet my whole life.

I noticed as we were pulling up to the mansion that two people had come out of the front door and were walking towards us. They were radiant. It was as if they shined with the purest of white. They were certainly set apart from other people. They were of the highest level of royalty. I noticed that with each step they took towards me my focus changed. The closer they got, the narrower my vision was.

When they were about twenty feet from me, my focus was directed to the eyes of the son. Suddenly, something inside me awakened, and it felt like it wanted to break out of me. I said to myself, *Just settle down, control yourself, don't get so emotional. Oh my God I feel like there is a volcano inside me ready to erupt. I can't hold it back!*

I fell to my knees on the carriage floor and began singing to the father and the son with my hands in the air. I was singing and praising them . In the middle of this praising , I could actually feel my brain kicking in. My mouth was singing praises, yet my brain was telling me to stop. It was saying, *you know you can't sing well, you know you look like a fool don't you. I'm sure Sue is embarrassed. I have to get myself under control.*

I seemed to come out of this and noticed that my brain was just going wild, calling me an absolute, out-of-control fool. Then I heard another voice telling me what a great freedom I had. I realized my response of praise was the greatest greeting I could give the King and his son.

Wow, I guess I couldn't have planned it any better. As I began to get up off the floor, I noticed my wife was lying on the seat. My eyes were drawn to her face. Her eyes were closed, and her face was glowing white. Then suddenly my focus changed; it was as if my eyes could see inside of her. I realized that I was seeing, what she was experiencing.

I saw an amazing thing. The King and his son had both wrapped their arms around her heart. I heard my brain again kick in and tell me that this was completely ridiculous. Then something in me rose up and spoke to my brain and told it to *shut up, you have nothing to say about this*. I agreed with that and under my breath told my brain to shut up. Instantly it was quiet again and I was able to see what was going on in my wife.

I saw an acceptance being placed in her heart; she had struggled with rejection for as long as I had known her. I saw security being placed in her heart, she was always so fearful of everything. I saw encouragement placed it her heart; it seemed like in the past it didn't take much for her to get discouraged . I was thinking H*mmm... they must have known her pretty well. Amazing!*

Then she got up and sat on the seat in a daze. I looked over at the King and His son who were standing near the door of the carriage. I thought they were probably wondering what was going on with their crazy guests. But as I looked into their faces I realized they would be happy to stand there all day if necessary. They seemed to enjoy watching our reactions to them.

I reached my hands toward Sue, and she grabbed them. I softly asked her if she was ready to get up. She said she was. I thought to myself, *there has been a lot of communication that has already taken place between the four of us without a word ever being spoken.* I assisted her as she began to stand. Then I saw the King's son open the carriage door, and the King reached out his hand to my wife and assisted her as she got off.

I could tell they had a genuine love for both of us. That really made me feel good. As they walked with us toward the mansion, I really felt like my wife and I were the guests of honor as the carriage driver had stated. We had never felt this way before. I heard my brain say, *"Yeah, that won't last long. As soon as they get you in the door you will get the sales pitch, like everyone does."*

I understood what he meant, but for some reason I knew it would be different this time. When we approached the door the son started to open it and the king said, "I am honored to have you both as our guests."

I thought, *REALLY?*^#?*

I was still wondering what we had done to be so honored. With this welcome, we both stepped inside . We were stunned as we tried to take in all the magnificence and beauty. I heard Sue say in a soft voice, "I have never seen such beauty. It's as if each piece..........."

I think her mouth quit working as I saw her eyes scanning everything. It seemed like it was an hour or more before we could even take our next step. I realized that up to now, every single step we took since we entered this town took us to a place that was beyond our realm of imagination. It was constant, over and over again. I would feel so inadequate to   explain this.

The King said, "I would like for you to be my guests for supper tonight, and after that I have planned a celebration in both your honors."

We both smiled and thanked him but again that question rose up in me, *what have we done that was so great to deserve this?* We were just ordinary people who lived ordinary lives. He then told his son to escort us to the guest room where we could rest and freshen up.

So we followed the son, who escorted us through several hallways. There were rooms off them and many large windows that overlooked the most beautiful gardens filled with every kind of flowers, singing birds, and other animals. I had never seen such creativity. I was so fascinated that for a few moments I had forgot where we were going. We had arrived at our room. The son opened the door to the guest room and invited us to step inside. Then he said to just relax and enjoy ourselves. We both thanked him as he left, closing the door behind him.

CHAPTER 4

CAN YOU BELIEVE THIS

I looked at Sue and said, "Can you believe this?"

She was unable to talk, but as we looked at each other we suddenly broke out into laughter. It was crazy-- every time we looked at each other we broke into laughter again.

When Sue gained her composure she said, "I feel so full of life!"

I told her I knew what she meant, and again we broke out in laughter. A while later we were able to talk. I told her, "This whole thing is absolutely crazy. Look at us, honey. We are nobody, just ordinary folks. I can't even think of any great things we have done in our lives that would even deserve recognition, can you?"

I was surprised by her answer. She said, "Well I can't think of anything for myself, but I can think of one for you."

I really would like to have been honored for something, I thought, so I responded to her by saying, "Well, that's cool. What is it?"

She looked directly at me and said, "Well, honey, for whatever reason I found it difficult to tell you this before, but I've always honored you for your faithfulness to me and our kids. You always worked hard for us. We were never without. I saw how you loved our kids and spent valuable time with them. I always knew that when you were driving that truck for days on end you would be faithful. I respected that, and it allowed me to make love with you every weekend knowing I was your special gift from God."

I was blown away! I never saw it that way. I just always felt guilty because I was gone so much. I said to myself, "I needed that."

I looked at her and said, "Honey, I also have something that I have been holding back for many years. I really don't know why I couldn't say this before. I have both honored and cherished you for your gentleness towards me and our kids. You had a way of smoothing out my rough edges. You brought peace in our home when I was just angry and wanting to lash out at the kids. Every time I got in my truck to take off, knowing I was leaving my family for five days, I would feel so guilty. But then I would think of you, and I knew that our family would be fine. You see, I've always known that you were God's gift to me. Every morning I thanked God for you."

Tears came to her eyes as she moved closer to me. I just opened my arms and welcomed her to me. We hugged like we had never hugged before. We both had a deep loyalty and love for each other. We were so blessed. I said, " WOW, what a day we have had!" She agreed and we both went to bed and snuggled and peacefully went to sleep.

Sometime later we woke up, then Sue said, "Honey, this is the first time that I can remember getting out of bed feeling completely rested, and full of vitality and life."

I agreed and was thinking about how great it was to see her so full of life. *She's such a beautiful woman*, I thought to myself. Than I realized that we had to go to supper. I started rushing around trying to find a clock to see what time it was.

"Honey," she asked," what are you doing?"

I replied, "I don't want to be late for this supper we are supposed to go to. What time does it start? Where's the clock?"

Then she said, "Honey, please stop. Just settle down for a minute."

Then I remembered what I had told her earlier about bringing a peace when I got worked up. Just like always she helped me to settle down.

"Okay ,honey I'm settled down. Now what time is it?"

She giggled and said, "We are in Godsville. Do you remember them telling us a time?"

"No, I don't. Ha... I guess you're right."

She said, "That's because there is no time here."

I was puzzled. "It sure is different here. I did notice that no one

37

seemed to be in a rush. Honey, how can there not be time? How would you know when to meet someone around here? Can you tell me?"

She said, "Well, I'm really not sure. The only thing I can say is when it's time to meet, we will all know it."

I agreed but didn't really understand it. As we began to get ready, I realized that we didn't bring any extra clothes with us. I thought, *this is going to be interesting*. I watched while Sue was drying off after stepping out of the shower. She was so full of life without a care in the world. I loved seeing her that way.

I remembered how it was when I enjoyed doing things to her just to make her mad--then I would tell her how cute she looked when she was mad. For some reason I didn't want to do that to her anymore. I needed to shower, but first I wanted to see her reaction when she realized she didn't have clothes to wear or makeup or whatever else she used to pretty up.

As she walked out of the bathroom she asked, "Bill, what do you plan to wear tonight?"

There was a pause as I thought, *she doesn't realize there are no clothes.*

I said, "I'm not sure yet, honey."

She said, "Well, I sure love you in your black suit and red tie."

 I said, "Okay, I'll wear that for you."

I thought, *she better be thinking about what she's going to wear.* She never said a word as she walked over to what I thought was a door to a small closet. When she opened the door, I saw a very large room full of beautiful clothing. She walked in and sorted through hundreds of outfits. I watched as she tried on one outfit after another. There were mirrors all over the place for her to see herself from every angle. She was having a great time. I thought, *I don't remember her going in that closet before. How did she know there were clothes in there?*

 I stepped inside the closet with her. I was amazed. In the closet, I saw all her favorite dresses. I looked more closely and saw several that I had bought her for Christmas. What in the world was going on?

I couldn't take it anymore so I said, "Honey, how did you know these clothes were in here?"

She confidently said, "Well, actually I didn't. All I knew was when I needed my clothes they would be there for me."

I responded, " Oh, okay."

Hmmm.... I thought to myself. *I don't get it. She has to know something I don't.* Well obviously she did because she was doing fine. *But what about me? I don't see anymore closets in this place. Where are my clothes?*

I searched everywhere, and there were none to be found. I walked back in the closet where Sue was nearly dressed. I was happy for her but still wondering about my clothes. I realized that she still had to fix her hair and put her makeup on, so I decided to look through the whole place to find it.

I looked everywhere possible; there was no makeup to be found.

Then she asked me, "Are you going to wear your black suit, honey?"

I said, " Yes, dear, I am. "

My brain was spinning with questions. I just couldn't figure this whole thing out. Then Sue walked out of the closet, approached me with a big smile, and said, "Well, how does this look?"

She was stunningly beautiful. I couldn't respond; I could only stare at her. She than said while walking away, "I guess I'll do my hair and makeup now. Why don't you put your suit on while I finish up? You look so handsome in it."

I had to sit down on the edge of the bed. My brain was going crazy. I looked all around the room wondering where I was going to find my clothes. Then I looked at Sue, and she was just enjoying this place and all it had to offer. I wanted to enjoy it just like she was, but I didn't know where my clothes were. I started shaking my head from side to side as fast as I could to see if I still had a brain in there. This had to be a dream; it couldn't be real. I found myself pinching my leg, and it did hurt.

I continued to just sit there; I didn't know what to do. A short time later, Sue walked back in the room and stood about ten feet away. She started turning around in circles and asked, "Well, how do I look?"

I was mesmerized by her beauty. It was a beauty I had never seen before. A short time later I thought, *something isn't right here.* As I sat on the edge of the bed and I look down at myself and said in a very low voice, "All I have is my dirty underwear."

I was lost and didn't know what to do. Then I looked again at her. She was so beautiful, so full of life, she looked like she was twenty six years old. Everything around her was beyond beautiful. It was like she was shining. I got up and walked over to a full-length mirror. I stood there and looked at myself, and my dirty underwear. I started talking to myself saying, *What is wrong? I can't find my clothes, I'm going to have to wear my dirty underwear, I can't even find the soap to take a shower or a towel to dry off.*

As I was talking to myself, she slowly walked up behind me and gently placed her arms on my shoulders. I felt such a peace come over me. She pressed her body tight against mine as she wrapped her arms around my waist. I just closed my eyes for a moment and experienced a calm and peaceful feeling penetrating deep within me. I opened my eyes for a second, looked into the mirror, and saw that her eyes were also closed. She was so peaceful. She had always been peaceful but nothing like this. Somehow we both opened our eyes at the same time, and we were looking in the mirror. I just knew I needed what she had.

Then she said, "Go shower and get your suit on."

I said, "Yep, it's that time." I knew something was different about me. I didn't understand it, but that was okay. Just before stepping into the shower, I realized there was no soap or shampoo--not even a towel--but I thought, *that's fine I'm just going to shower anyway.*

When it came time for me to get the soap, I reached over to where the soap should be and sure enough it was there. I thought, *Wow, that's cool!* I picked it up along with a wash cloth and proceeded to clean myself. Then, when I needed the shampoo, I just reached for it in the location I thought it should be and again it was there. I thought, *This is so cool, I think I'm getting the hang of things around here.*

Bill didn't realize it, but Sue was watching him the whole time. Sue thought to herself, *he is beginning to learn to trust instead of having to figure everything out.* She was encouraged as she watched Bill reach for the towel as he stepped out of the shower, but as soon as he felt the towel she heard him say to himself, " I think I've figured this place out."

Sue just shook her head as she thought... "*I can see it all now*". Let the show begin.

Sue took a seat in a chair in the corner of the room. She knew Bill very well, and she planned to observe as he demonstrated his new confidence. Sue could see that he was off in his own little world and he didn't realize that she was watching. She could see his confidence was growing rapidly as he discovered his clean underwear, his deodorant, his razor and everything else he needed. Each time he discovered something, his confidence soared. Just before he walked out of the bathroom, Sue heard him say to himself, *I've got this place all figured out.*

Chapter 5

THERE'S A PEACOCK IN THE ROOM

Bill started to walk out of the bathroom. With each step he took, I could see his pride soar. His walk started to turn into a strut. I just had to giggle softly. I was enjoying myself too much to disturb him. I watched as he strutted over to the mirror and admired himself as he said, "Look, everyone, I know where to find my clean underwear."

I was doing everything I could to hold back the laughter. He had no clue how silly he looked--a grown man standing in front of the mirror with only his clean underwear on and feeling so proud of it. He began to strut all around the room. As his pride grew, his strut became more dramatic. He looked like a strutting peacock. I couldn't control myself. I burst out laughing. Because he didn't realize I was watching, he seemed to be embarrassed.

Bill immediately stopped and said in a not-so-happy tone, "How long have you been watching me?"

I replied, "The whole time. It was quite the show."

Bill said, "Okay, that's fine. I'm glad you enjoyed yourself, but aren't you also proud of my ability to figure out the system here.... Did you see me get the soap?..."

Sue didn't respond.

Bill said, "Well, how about the shampoo?"

Sue didn't respond. Bill was starting to get upset at her. He really wanted her to say she was proud of him. Bill began to speak more loudly, wanting Sue's response. He said, "Don't you realize I discovered the wash rag, too?... and don't forget the towel. Don't you remember as I was stepping out of the shower I got the towel? Don't you remember?" Again Sue didn't respond.

Bill was really starting to get mad. He said, "What about my clean underwear? That was certainly a big deal. What about the deodorant and my razor and cologne and stuff?"

Sue could see that he was very frustrated as he was nearing the end of his discoveries. When Bill had run out of things to say there was silence. Bill knew that if he just remained silent and glare into her eyes that she would have to give him an answer. He figured at any moment she would have to say the words that he wanted to hear, "Yes, I'm proud of you, honey."

Bill kept staring into Sue's eyes, keeping the pressure on. He watched every little movement of her face and eyes in anticipation. There was still total silence in the room.

Bill knew that the first one to speak was the loser. He could see that she was close to saying those words. Bill kept the pressure on.

Then suddenly he noticed a slight moment in her lips and it happened. She said, "Bill, I don't have give you any more pride because you already have more than you need!"

Bill was stunned; he didn't even know how to respond. Now every emotion kicked in, his brain started shooting rapid fire questions and yelling, *I don't understand!* Bill's boat was rocked!

After a few minutes, he apologized for his attitude. Then he asked Sue, "Can you help me understand what you meant by that statement?"

Sue replied, "Bill, I respect you very much, but there are times when I am able to see things that can cause you harm. I would love to be able to openly and honestly talk about them instead of us getting mad at each other. I loved watching you make the discoveries that you did, but when you thought you had the whole thing figured out is when I realized that your over confidence would lead you to something destructive. Honey, it's not about figuring things out, it's just about trusting."

Bill caught what she was saying and stated, "You're so right. My brain always wants to figure things out. I realize that has caused me many problems throughout my life. I'm so sorry."

He gave Sue a big hug and thanked her for helping him. She said, "Bill, I think you are now ready to discover your nice black suit and   red tie."

Bill walked over to a door that was next to her closet door and opened it, and there was a huge walk-in closet full of beautiful clothes.

Sue heard Bill say, "WOW! Where did this come from?"

Then he paused and said, "I guess I can't figure it out, and I'm better off that way. Trusting is much easier anyway."

Sue watched as Bill had a great time trying on all sorts of clothes. A while later Sue walked in and looked around. Then she started to laugh.

I asked, "What's so funny?"

Sue responded, "Some things never change."

I looked down and saw all the clothes I had just tried on were thrown everywhere. We both started laughing . Then we came together and hugged. It was a beautiful thing. Oh how we had bonded so much in just this one day!

As I was getting ready, I felt relaxed and ready to enjoy the evening. My shoes were shined and the suit was pressed and everything was perfect. I was looking in the mirror to make sure my tie was straight before I presented myself to Sue. I said to myself, "I'm going to be picture perfect."

When I had everything just right, I walked out to where she was sitting. She was looking at her hands and fingernails and seemed happy with them. As soon as she realized I was in the room, she looked up at me. She immediately stood up and stared. I knew I had made a big impact on her, so I decided to take it a step farther and do that "circle thing", like she had done. Now she could experience my perfection from every angle.

She was so pleased with how I looked. I was so proud of the job I did to look perfect. I knew this was a perfect Romeo and Juliet moment. She reached out her hands toward me, and I gently held them. We were now face to face.

She said," I'm so proud of you. "

Her smile brought great joy to me. Then she said, "You are so handsome."

As our bodies drew closer together, I said, "I love you with everything that's in me. I need you, and I couldn't live without you."

As we drew closer I put my arms around her waist as she wrapped her arms around my neck. I knew that a beautiful kiss was coming. As our lips touched I could taste her sweetness. It was so beautiful. I was so consumed by her. Then suddenly I could feel her hands straightening the back of my collar. Then she said, "You really do need me, don't you?"

I agreed and asked, "Well honey, are you ready to go?"

She replied, "Yes, it's time."

Chapter 6

SOON TO BE MY CLOSEST FRIENDS

So we left our room to go to the dining room. I was so excited and had visualized what this supper with the King was going to be like. I said, "Honey, do you realize what we are going to?"

She said," Yes, to supper."

I said, "No, don't you get it? We are going to a supper with Royalty. I can picture it. There will be a long banquet table that probably seats thirty or forty people. The table alone probably costs $250,000.00. There will be servants and probably a roasted hog with an apple in its mouth, the best wine, and more exotic side dishes then we can imagine. I envision the King showing us some of his priceless artifacts and gifts from other kings and royalty. He will probably explain more about his town and the great fortune we would have by moving here. Obviously he's doing something right because the economy appears to be doing well. It will be interesting to listen to some of his stories about himself. Don't you think?"

There was a short pause as Sue thought, *here we go again, he's figuring everything out.* Then she calmly replied, "Well, I guess we'll know soon enough. "

As we approached the dining room, we could see that the double doors at the entrance were already open. When we reached the entrance, we were greeted by the King and his son. I noticed that their clothing was much more casual than I had expected. They seemed to be relaxed and truly delighted to have us as guests.

As they escorted us to the dining room table, I was surprised because it was not what I had envisioned. The table was a high quality table, but it was just a round table that comfortably seated four. When we approached, they pulled out the chairs for us.

Once we were seated, I looked all around to see where the servants were. When I realized there were none I asked, "Where are the servants?"

The King stated, "They have the day off."

I responded by saying ,"Okay?," That surprised me because I knew this was suppose to be a special occasion.

The King asked, "Are you both refreshed and relaxed?"

My wife said yes and thanked them for the beautiful room.

The King said, "I would like to share one story with you before we begin eating."

Bill thought, *well, at least I was right about one thing--he was going to tell us a story about himself.*

The King began by asking, "Do you remember about ten years ago when you were trying to sell your house on Maple Street so you could purchase the house in Indianapolis?"

My wife said, "Yes, I do. How about you, honey?"

I said, "Certainly do! How could I forget? It looked like we were going to lose a lot of money in the deal. I remember how much I racked my brain to try to figure a way to sell our house in such a depressed market. We had a beautiful house to buy

54

in Indianapolis, but we only had thirty days to sell our Maple Street house to get the new one. I remember we had four or five offers on the house, but they were so low that there was no way we could do it. Sure, I remember that, it was a stressful time."

Sue said, " Yes, but I kept saying things would be fine, just let God take care of them."

I replied, "Well, that is true, but it was really hard for me to do that.

Then the King said," I understand.   But when your buyer came, wasn't that two days before your deadline?"

I said, "Yeah....?" as I wondering how he knew that.

Then the King said, "If I'm right, didn't you sell it for your asking price?"

I said, " Yeah...?"

Then the king said, "I remember celebrating that sale with you. Let's eat."

I thought, *he sure knows a lot about us.*

As I got up to walk over to the buffet table, the King said, "Just stay in your seat. I'll get it for you. It's the least I could do for you."

Then the son got up to get the food for Sue. I just looked over at her. She seemed content and peaceful.

I asked her, "Aren't you wondering how they know so many details about our lives?"

She said, "No, honey, I'm not even thinking about it. "

I asked her if she had ever heard of the "beast" she said no."

"Well," I replied, "it's a huge computer located somewhere. It gathers personal information on people all over the world. I'm sure they have the connections to tap into it and get all our information."

Sue replied, "I don't think so, dear."

"Well how else would he know these things?" I asked.

She replied," I don't know for sure. Let's just enjoy ourselves and have fun together. I think the King could be a fun-loving guy if we let him. They both enjoy being with us. "

When they returned with our food, it looked very good, although I was surprised that it wasn't super fancy. The King asked what we wanted to drink. I asked him what he had, and he said, "Whatever you want."

I was thirsty, so I said, "Water, please."

Then he left the room and returned with it. As we were eating, the King brought up the time we had nearly missed our plane on our wedding night. It was one of those stories that are only funny years later. We all laughed, and that led us to many more funny stories of our life.

This really got me going. I loved to tell funny stories about my wife and me. Usually I was the guy with the pie in the face. They laughed for hours at my stories. I realized how much fun I was having. I had never been with someone who loved to hear my stories for hours. We literally sat there and enjoyed each other until I completely ran out of stories to tell.

The King and his son never got tired of my stories. I told so many of them that I realized several of them I had told twice and one even three times. That didn't matter to them. They actually seemed to enjoy them even more the second and third time around. They would ask me questions in the middle of the story, and each time that led to more laughter.

I got so sweaty I had to loosen my tie and remove my sport coat and later I even rolled my sleeves up. We laughed so hard that all four of us were rolling on the ground holding our stomachs begging to stop. What a night!

Chapter 7

THE HIGH VALUE OF LIFE

Afterward, the King asked if we were ready to be honored at the awards ceremony. I looked at my wife and asked, "Are you ready to go now, or do you want to freshen up?"

She stated that she was ready to go. I looked at the King and asked him, "Who did you say was being honored tonight?

The King replied, "You and Sue! It's a celebration of your lives!"

I could see in his eyes that he truly meant what he said. I replied, "Okay, but I'm not sure what we are going to celebrate other than our arrival here."

The King said , "Yes, that's certainly worth celebrating as well."

They led us to a massive auditorium with seven levels of seating. My wife pointed at the ceiling which, had to be one hundred yards long. It was a stunningly beautiful--all hand painted with precious stones inlaid throughout. It was so beautiful that it brought tears to my eyes. I saw my wife actually weeping at it's beauty.

The King and his son escorted us onto the stage which was located in the front portion of the auditorium. In the center of the stage was a small raised platform, which was covered in an expensive-looking carpet. It was a royal blue in color with what looked like flakes of gold scattered throughout, so it sparkled. On the platform were two chairs that were made of gold and precious stones.

I whispered to Sue, "Honey, do you realize it would take me ten lifetimes of driving my rig to pay for one of those chairs."

She just nodded her head in agreement. Then I whispered to her again, "I think the two chairs are probably for the King and his son, but I don't see where we are going to sit."

She replied in a very low whisper, "Would you just be quiet?"

"Yes, dear," I answered.

A few seconds later I whispered to her, "What's on that table next to the chairs?"

She replied in a stern voice, "Please be quiet."

Again I replied, "Yes, dear. "

The King and his son assisted us in stepping up onto the raised platform. Then the king said to us, "Please, take your seats," as they attempted to assist us.

Both Sue and I stiffened. The King said, "Please, these are your seats. "

I wasn't good enough to sit in such a chair. I couldn't help myself, so I told the King, "I'm not good enough."

Then Sue followed by saying, "I'm not good enough either."

Both the King and his son gently told us, "It's okay. Just have a seat."

Their words of encouragement were very powerful, and they helped us to accept the seats of honor. I looked at Sue, and she followed my lead to sit. As I sat down, I felt something growing inside of me. The feeling started in my toes and it was working its way up from there. When it got just above my knees, I happened to look up. I saw the King and his Son standing in front of me. My eyes caught the king's eyes. I realized that he was giving me his royalty.

The royalty continued to rise, and when it reached the top of my stomach I felt something jump inside of me-- my spirit and his spirit connecting. The feeling continued working it's way up; I could feel it consuming every part of me. When it reached my heart, I felt a cleansing. Then as it continued it consumed my tongue, then my eyes, I could see everything clearly. It was as if I saw beauty for the first time.

Finally, the King's royalty consumed my brain. I felt so different, like my whole thinking process had changed. I was absolutely shocked. I saw everything out of new eyes, and my heart was full of compassion. Everything I saw was full of beauty, and even my own words seemed to bring life to me. I knew I had just experienced a freedom I didn't even know existed. I was free to love and free to receive love. I felt young and alive. I realized that the real me was my spirit. For the first time, I had broken free and experienced true life, and I was amazed!

Now I knew that the King was God, and his Son was Jesus. They were the two closest friends who had the messenger call me. Now I could plainly see how much they loved Sue and me. They had planned this day for all of our lives, and we never had a clue. I just gave them praise and thanks for all they had done for us.

Then Jesus said to me, "This day has made it all worth the price I paid."

I couldn't believe it. He felt more blessed, yet we were the ones who got all the benefits. WOW.... what a love!

Then I looked over at Sue, who was still sitting in the chair next to me. I could see that she received the same thing I did.

Suddenly I heard my brain starting up again, doubting what had happened. I just giggled and said, "Leave now in the name of Jesus," and he shut his mouth and never returned.

I couldn't deny what had happened to me. The spirit inside of me had experienced a rebirth. I had been set free from the captivity that sin keep me in, which had caused me to believe lies about myself and God, resulting in much destruction to myself and the relationship with my wife and others.

In the past, I remembered asking myself, *why is it so hard to love and be loved?* I now understood that the power of sin, along with my lack of knowledge and understanding of God, had robbed me from knowing his goodness.. *WOW.... how little I really knew about life, when I thought I knew so much.*

Enough of that, I thought, *my spirit is no longer captive to that evil kingdom. Now I'm free and I'm experiencing a new life that is untouched by sin.*

I asked Jesus, "How can I repay you?"

Jesus replied, "Don't concern yourself with that now. Just receive it and enjoy it. After all, this is just your first day with us."

Jesus continued by saying, "Bill, I receive an abundance of joy just watching and listening to you and Sue."

I thought to myself, *I have to express my love back.* However, there were no words I could say that would be able to express my love and appreciation for what he had done on the cross. The only response that could satisfy me in expressing my love was to worship him.

Sue and I looked at each other, and at the same time we fell to our knees and together worshipped God and his Son Jesus. It was a wonderful experience of giving back to them. Sometime later, we got up off the floor and sat down in our seats. I couldn't believe all that happened to us since we first sat down.

We watched as God walked over to the table next to our chairs. He picked up what looked like a royal scarf and walked back and stood in front of Sue. He looked into her eyes and said, "I'm honored to present to you this royal scarf. It represents your faithfulness in trusting me throughout your life. This trust enabled me to use you, to express my love to those whose hearts were broken. You will wear this for eternity as symbol of my honor to you. Thank you for trusting me."

I could see she was very touched by receiving the scarf. I thought back to countless times that Sue reached out to families who were left with nothing after natural disasters and house fires. She always led the way and organized teams of people to respond to those who needed love and support.

Then God walked back over to the table again. This time he picked up a beautiful set of rings and he walked back and stood in front of Sue. I could see that she couldn't believe there was anything else to be honored for. God held up a beautiful set of rings. One had huge, sparkling diamonds on it. They appeared to be the source of light instead of a reflection of light. God gently reached for her hand, and as he was placing the rings on her finger he said, "I am honoring you with these rings for both your faithfulness to me and your husband. You were faithful to me when you received him by becoming his wife. The ring also represents your faithfulness to Bill. You were his helpmate for life, as I had planned. Now wear these rings of honor for eternity. I thank you for your obedience. "

I realized that every award she received was revealing to me who she really was as a person. I couldn't believe I hadn't seen that before.

Then God walked back to the table and removed a beautiful gold necklace and again brought it to Sue. Then God said, "Sue, I'm honored to present to you this gold necklace. It represents the great sacrifices you made to help both your family and others outside your family when they lost a loved one. "

God continued by saying, "I specifically remember a time, shortly after losing your children in that tragic accident, when you reached out to Lydia and her children. They were overwhelmed by the loss of Joe. Lydia was having a difficult time seeing her children crying and saying, 'Please give me my daddy back.' I was so proud when I saw you reach out to them even while you were still suffering from your own great loss. This necklace represents your beauty as a mother of many."

Then God gently placed it around her neck. "You will wear this for eternity as a symbol of honor." I watched as God was shedding some tears himself for the pain that mothers have experienced with the loss of a loved one.

God said, "It was because of your love and compassion that I was able to show my love to them. Thank you for doing that for me." Sue had many tears running down her face as she was being so greatly honored. I saw God gently wiping them away.

Then I saw what appeared to be angels, five of them. They were directed by God to Sue, who still was weeping. These angels were very peaceful, calm, and loving, and they were ministering to her. God asked them to walk with her and to take very good care of her. As they escorted her off the stage, I felt that she was in good hands.

Once they were gone, both God and Jesus looked at me with big smiles. I could tell they were so happy that this day of celebration had become a reality. I just stopped for a moment and thought about how they had already given Sue and me so much more than we could ever have imagined--and the only thing they received from us was US! Unbelievable!

Than I heard Jesus tell God how much Sue had blessed them in her life. God said, "Yes, she brought me great joy."

Next, God walked back to the table and picked up a pair of golden shoes and stood in front of me, holding them. They were stunning; I'd never seen shoes so beautiful. I listened closely as God said, "I am honored to present to you these shoes. They represent the personal sacrifices you made by leaving your family every week for days at a time. You travelled the whole country. Everywhere you went, you left a footprint. I recall how outgoing you were with other drivers and their families. You always went out of your way to greet them and make them feel welcome. It didn't matter to you if they were white or black or foreigners. You just made them feel welcome. You had a way of starting conversations, and when they were comfortable enough to share about themselves, you became a good listener. You faithfully acted on your desire to help them. That desire was given to you by me. I received much joy from you when I would speak to your heart to bless them with money and you gave it.

"Do you remember two Christmases ago outside Chicago? There was a driver who had run out of gas on I-94 during rush hour, and you stopped to help him. His name was Dan, and he just finished a drop and was headed to his ex-wife's house in Portage. His five-year-old son, Tommy, was there anxiously waiting for his daddy to arrive with his Christmas present. You see Dan's ex-wife had set a time deadline for him to arrive. If you hadn't stopped to help, he wouldn't have been able to see his son. That day was so important to Dan and to Tommy. I was so happy when I saw the look on both their faces as Tommy was running out to meet his daddy.

"So I am honored to present to you these shoes. They are a symbol of your personal sacrifice to bless others. Thank you for being faithful by using the gifts I placed in you."

Then God got down on his knees, removed my shoes, and carefully straightened my socks. Then he put the golden shoes on my feet. I experienced a special honor that could only come from being honored by the one who is most honored.

I looked him in the eyes and tried to thank him, but no words could come out. He just looked at me and said, "I understand."

He slowly got up off his knees and walked back to the table where he picked up a golden crown. When he knew I was ready, he walked back and stood in front of me. I thought, t*here is no way that I could ever deserve a crown.*

He stood there holding the crown at my eye level, then he asked, "Bill, have you ever seen anything that looked like this before?"

I quickly said, "No "

Then I paused for a moment as I thought. Then I said, "There is something familiar about it."

God asked," What's familiar about it?"

I was thinking, *where have I seen this before?* "I got it! That looks like the logo I used when I started my trucking business."

God replied, "Yep, that's right."

Then I said," I named my company, Crown Trucking Inc.!"

God asked, "Do you remember why you gave it that name?"

I responded with a short giggle, "It's kinda silly, but at that time I felt like Sue and I would be royalty someday."

God asked, "Does it seem silly now?"

I replied, " No, sir, it does not."

God said, "I am honored to present to you this golden royal crown for the leadership you demonstrated throughout your life. I created you to lead people. You led them faithfully through your patience, love and encouragement. Now if you look straight ahead, I have something to show you."

God stepped aside and a large theater screen appeared. It started showing the good deeds I had done in my life. I was shocked; it was as if I went back in time and the deeds were as real to me as when I was doing them. I noticed one big difference, though--I was seeing it through different eyes and that allowed me to receive the full benefit of joy that wasn't possible when I actually was doing it. I was able to see for the first time the true value of my life. I really did make a difference. I couldn't believe how difficult it had been for me to place any value on my life.

As soon as the pictures stopped, I felt the golden royal crown being placed on my head from God himself. I was able to receive the full reward of the honor. God said, "Bill, do you now understand how I look at you and your life?"

I said," Yes, I do."

God replied, "I wish others did as well."

Chapter 8

MY GIFT TO YOU

As I was sitting there I was overwhelmed by emotions. Then out of the corner of my eye I got a glimpse of something very beautiful. However, when I looked around, I didn't see anything. I thought, *did I imagine this, or did I really see something?*

Then I watched as the royal stage curtains opened. Behind them stood the most beautiful and mysterious creature. I didn't know what it was, but I was fascinated by it. I admired its beauty from head to toe.

As it started to walk toward me, I began to focus on its movement. It was a movement I was familiar with. Then I looked at its hair and I realized the hair looked familiar as well. As it walked closer to me, I looked at the face and I caught an expression that I was familiar with. Then I looked into it's eyes, and it was as if my whole inner being had awakened.

As the creature walked closer, I began mourning as if I had suffered a great loss. The pain began to subside as a hope began to rise in me. I grabbed onto the hope and held on as if my life depended on it. Every step it took my hope would rise.

I raised myself up from the chair as the hope continued to rise. I was nearly to the point of begging as I said, "Can it be? Oh, please, can it be?" I was so fascinated with this beautiful creature. What quickly passed through me was the thought that I had a fascination once before and it was for Sue. Oh dear God, could it be her? I felt the hope surge as I said that.

Then the creature looked at me and smiled. I began saying, "I know that smile! I know that smile! It is her! It is Sue!" At that very moment she stopped walking and just stood there looking at me with the most beautiful smile I had ever seen.

She said, "Yes, my love, it is me."

I was overwhelmed with joy. My beautiful wife was back! When I looked at her, it felt like she was presenting herself to me as a gift, a gift of beauty. I stood there staring at her, as if my eyes were an open door to receive the beauty she had to give. I could tell she loved to pour out her beauty and experience the joy that I was receiving from it.

I didn't move as her beauty continued to flow in me. My whole life I had longed to be filled with her beauty. My eyes continued to take her in--her face was radiant, her body was as smooth as silk, and her eyes could see in me. It was as if she knew the level of her beauty inside me.

She was so full of life. Her hair was golden and soft as it flowed so smoothly in the soft wind. She was so gentle and peaceful. Then, as if she knew I had received all her beauty, she began slowly walking toward me. I was so overwhelmed by her beauty that I felt I could burst.

In response, I began walking toward her. All we could do is look into each other's eyes. I could see her heart through her eyes. I saw a woman presenting her beauty to me so that I may cherish it, love it, enjoy it, and be satisfied as her man. There was about ten feet between us when we both stopped, still staring in each other's eyes. Then we heard God's voice say, "Bill, I now present to you your greatest gift. That is Sue, your woman of beauty."

We both reached out our arms and ran towards each other. When we finally touched and embraced, our whole inner beings leaped out and entered into the other. At that very moment we became one. We couldn't stop embracing each other. Our love flowed back and forth like nothing I had experienced before. It was as if we were now free to give love and free to receive love. This was the place we were looking for.

Both God and Jesus walked up to us smiling. Sue and I embraced them and thanked them for this miraculous day. Sue couldn't stop saying, "Thank you both so very much."

The interesting thing was there were no words we could say that would satisfy our deep feelings of appreciation. So together we knelt down before them and worshipped them. This was the only thing we could do to truly release our love, honor, and thanks for what they had done.

Then God said, "Today we have celebrated your lives, and you have brought us great joy, but tomorrow we will take you to the place that we have prepared for you.

Jesus took our hands and began directing us back to our room. While walking there I looked over at Sue and said, "Honey, we walked this hallway once before and so many things have happened since then. It was as if we were gone a thousand years instead of one day."

Jesus just watched us as we were enjoying each other. He knew this would last for eternity. We arrived and as Jesus was opening the door he said, "Enjoy each other in your new life, and tomorrow you will discover your new place in heaven."

He then walked out of the room and closed the door behind him. We just stood there looking at each other, I said, "We were just ordinary people, living ordinary lives, and because of them we are extraordinary people, living extraordinary lives. What else can we say?"

Sue said, "I have something to add."

"And what's that, my beautiful, charming, sexy, gorgeous wife?" I asked.

Sue stated, "Some things never do change."

I asked, " What do you mean? I thought everything had changed."

Sue giggled as she said, "Well, why are your dirty underwear from yesterday, still on the floor?"

I looked at them and remembered the story behind them. "Yeah, Sue that's one of those stories that are only funny years after they happened."

We laughed, hugged each other again, and went to bed.

Chapter 9

A VERY BIG DAY

Morning had come and Sue had just woken up. As she lay there, she realized how great it was to have a new day ahead of her. She was so excited to see what God had prepared for them. She thought, *I feel like a six-year-old on Christmas morning sneaking into Mom and Dad's bedroom, looking for any indication that they might be waking up.*

Sue was anxious to start the day. Then it happened--Bill rolled over in the bed. That was enough. She literally pounced on top of him and said, "It's going to be a beautiful day. Get up, get up."

Bill was startled for a second then remembered where he was. He said, "Honey, we are in heaven, right?"

She replied, "Yes, dear."

He said as he flew out of bed, "Then what are you doing lying around in   bed? Let's go."

She jumped out of bed and threw herself at him, and they hugged with big smiles on their faces.

Sue said, "This is going to be a big day."

Bill agreed and then asked, "Sue, you seem to have a little better understanding on how to operate up here. You know, like getting clothes when there aren't any and things like that. So maybe you can help me understand a little what God meant when he said tomorrow he would take us to the place he has prepared for us.

Sue thought for a moment then said, " I'm sorry, Bill. I don't think I can answer that directly, but there are a few things I think we can be confident in."

Bill replied, "Please tell me."

She said, "Well, let's just sort a few things out together and maybe it will help us."

Bill thought, *she has always been better at that than me.*

She started by saying, "We have no way of imagining what God will present to us today, but what we do have is yesterday.

Let's start by asking ourselves what we have learned about God himself. We certainly know him a lot better now."

Bill said, "That's true, but I need to say one thing before we go down this path."

Sue said, "Go ahead, Bill."

He thought for a short moment then he said, "You and I have spent a lot of time thinking and processing things together before, and many times we ended up with the wrong conclusions."

Sue agreed as Bill continued, " I realize how much different it is this time." Then Bill paused.

Sue encouraged him to continue. "Well, the difference is that we are not trying to figure out what's going to happen. Instead we are sharing with each other what we have learned about God."

Sue said, "Well, obviously you have learned something about him to have even made that statement, so let me have it you handsome critter. "

"Okay, honey," he said. "I know that he loves us both, and I can believe   that."

Sue asked, "What else?"

Bill replied, "I know he has everything to offer and all I can give him is me."

Sue replied, "Yeah, that's true, and God seems to be satisfied with that. Amazing! Anything else, dear?"

He replied, "Yes, one more thing, and then it's your turn. Not once did he ever tell us how bad we were. Before I always thought he was mad at me."

Sue said, " You're so right. I struggled with that as well. I always felt like I wasn't good enough to talk with him and if I tried he would probably just ignore me. How wrong I was!"

Bill said, "Can you imagine how different our lives could have been if we knew him like we do today?"

Sue said, "Wow! You're right--and to think we have only known him for one day.....Wow, that's incredible!"

We both sat for a minute trying to take in everything we had just discovered about God. Then Bill said, "Sue it's your turn. You haven't shared your discoveries yet."

Sue thought for a moment then said, "Bill, I just realized that we started this conversation by sharing what we have learned about God and who he is. Yesterday we didn't have a clue about what was going on. We didn't even know our closest friends were God and his son Jesus. This place was so different to us that we had to be led by them, and after they escorted us to where they wanted us, we would just watch and receive what they gave us. They sure were great at making us feel comfortable.

"God was very sensitive to how we felt that first day. Everything was so full of beauty, amazement, love and freedom. He put us at ease through his hospitality, his openness to listen, his humility, his honoring of us, his interest in our lives, and not bragging on his own. All he cared about was loving us. Honey, with all that you have discovered about who God actually is, how would you describe him?"

Bill thought for a moment then replied, "Well, Sue, I think of everything we discovered about him--his patience, his encouraging words, his understanding of us and of course his hospitality. He certainly always gave us the best he had. There are many more things that I could add, but really they are all just part of his great character. But to actually identify who He is, there is no word to describe him."

Then he paused; it looked like something was being revealed to him.

Sue said, "Well?......."

Bill asked as he was trying to switch boxes in his brain, "Well, what?"

"Well, who is He?" Sue asked.

Bill replied, "Love. He is Love! I just discovered that whoever was telling my brain that God was mad at me and I was never good enough--that's all a lie! We have believed a lie!"

Not a word was spoken for quite a long time. It was as if each of them were face to face in God's presence, and they were in their own personal and intimate conversations with him. This went on for hours. At times you would hear some soft weeping. At other times you would hear a short giggle. Then more silence.

Finally, Bill said   quietly, "I had no idea."

A while later Sue fell to her knees in a beautiful and intimate worship to God. It was a very powerful experience that would forever seal in them God's pure and true love. The atmosphere in the room was saturated with love, and every part of their bodies inside and out was consumed with His love.

Sometime later, God's presence slowly lifted from the room. At this point both Sue and Bill were laying face down on the floor and not moving. As they came out of it at the same time, they found themselves sitting face to face just three feet apart. They stared at each other for a minute.

Sue started to giggle as she thought, *What a sight he is.*

Then Bill started giggling as he thought, *what a sight she is.*

Sue began to laugh at Bill's appearance. He looked half asleep. His hair was standing straight up, and his eyes looked a little crooked with one open more than the other. He was a sight to behold.

Sue stated as she continued to laugh, "And I am stuck with you forever!"

Bill also started laughing and said, "Would you like for me to get you a mirror?"

Finally, they realized it was time to get ready for their big day. As they were getting up Bill said, "Boy, it's already been a great day."

Sue replied, "It sure has been. It's like the great things never stop."

As we were getting ready, I noticed Bill was enjoying his new discoveries. He was like a small child fascinated with a new toy. He was having fun, and I enjoyed watching him. When he was done showering, he reached for the towel and I could see and it was there. I could see that his confidence level was growing.

As he continues getting ready, I could see that he was becoming overly confident. I heard him softly talking to himself saying "I think I got it all figured out. Sure enough they were there as he started to put on his clean underwear, I could see his pride increasing as he believed, he had figured everything out.

After his underwear were on, he started strutting around the place like a proud peacock. I could tell he was looking at me out of the corner of his eye. He wanted to make sure I was looking at him. I acted like I didn't notice, and he kept doing the peacock walk.

Finally, he couldn't take it anymore. He stopped and looked at me and said, "What do you think?"

I knew it was my turn to play a game with him. I replied, "What do you mean?"

"Well...I was just wondering if you noticed anything different about me today?"

I replied, "well, let me think..." After a short pause I replied, "Yes, I do."

Bill said, "Well, tell me what it is."

I said, "Well... I can't quite put a handle on it... Let me think."

I could see that Bill was trying to be patient, but on the inside he was ready to burst, so I paused a little longer. Finally, he couldn't take it anymore. He said, "Now, Sue, don't play games with me. Tell me what you see is different about me today."

"Okay, Bill, there is an obvious change in you today as compared to yesterday."

Bill anxiously said, "Well, what is it?"

Sue said, "The biggest change I see today from yesterday is that today you're wearing clean underwear."

It was as if all the air was let out of his balloon. After Bill dealt with a few of his emotions, he said, "Here I was so proud that I had figured out how everything works around here. Didn't you see me discover my soap?"

She replied, "Yes, I did, and I was so happy for you."

Bill said, "Well, what about the shampoo?"

She replied, "I saw that ,too."

"Well, were you   proud of me?"

She said, "Yes, I was."

He sarcastically replied, "Well, you could have told me that."

Sue didn't respond.

Bill said, "Did you see me when I discovered the towel?"

She replied, "Yes I did honey."

He said, "Well?....... were you proud of me then?"

She replied, " I didn't have to be. You were getting proud enough on your own."

Bill wasn't sure what to say, so he just continued walking around the room in his underwear trying to process what she had said.

Sue watched him as he was walking. He had gone from a peacock strut to pacing back and forth. After a short while Bill asked, "Honey, I'm sorry for acting so proud. You have your way of stopping me in my tracks. I was kind of feeling pretty good about myself. I was figuring heaven out. Why wouldn't you let me keep going, at least a little while longer?"

Sue said, "Well, actually I did it for you, Bill. I didn't want you to have another awkward moment."

Bill asked, "What are you talking about?"

Sue said, "Well it was the peacock walk; you know the 'I got it all figured out walk.' I didn't want you to be standing in front of the mirror in your underwear talking to yourself again."

Bill didn't say anything for a moment, then after thinking about it he walked up to Sue, gave her a hug and, said, "Heaven is way too amazing for me to ever think I can figure it out."

Chapter 10

THE PLACE I HAVE PREPARED FOR YOU

There was a knock at the door, when we opened it there stood God and Jesus, with big smiles on their faces.

Sue stated, "I'm so happy just being with you both."

Bill said, "So am I."

God replied, "I'm so happy to be with you both. This is a day that my son and I have looked forward to for over sixty years. Are you ready?"

Then Jesus looked at Bill and said, "Where would you like to go?"

Bill was a little confused by Jesus's question, but after a short pause he said, "To the place you have prepared for us."

At that very instant, they were standing in front of a very large estate with beautiful rolling hills, lush green grass, and beautiful ornamental trees, as well as dozens of different types of fruit trees. There were bushes with every kind of berries. Everything was ripe and looked delicious.

There were flowers everywhere in every color imaginable. Sue said, "This is absolutely gorgeous. This is exactly what I've always desired. I love flowers! I love fresh fruit and berries."

As they were admiring the property, Bill began looking intently at a beautiful waterfall off to their right. Bill thought, "It looks like there could be a cave entrance behind the waterfalls."

Knowing what Bills thought was, God said "Bill, go check it out!"

Bill and Sue always loved caves; they had toured nearly every cave in the United States. As Bill walked in behind the waterfall, he yelled out, "I don't believe it!"

He stood there in amazement as Sue ran up to him. When she saw what was behind the waterfall, she nearly fainted. She saw a beautiful cave mansion that appeared to be endless. Bill and Sue had always talked about how cool it would be to live in a cave behind a waterfall. Bill looked at God and Jesus with tears in his eyes and said, "This is so far beyond anything I could have imagined. I don't know the words to say to express my appreciation."

All they could do was fall to their knees and worshipped them.

Sometime later they rose, still overwhelmed by God's goodness. Jesus took a silk cloth and wiped the tears from Sue's face. She tried to thank him, but no words came out. Jesus looked at her and said, " You are so very welcome."

Bill thought, *my whole life I had many people say they loved me but they rarely ever show it. God says I love you by continually showing us his love. Everything about him is love. God is love. He is so amazing!*

Then Jesus said, "My father and I received great joy when we prepared this place for you. We watched both of you as you reached out to hurting people and expressed my father's love to them. My father placed these people in the paths of your lives, and you faithfully showed them my love."

Bill felt humbled and said, "I gave so little, but you gave so much."

God said, "It wasn't a little thing to me. I loved them so much, and without you I couldn't have let them know. Many times I am unable to tell them, so I can show them only through someone. Did you know that throughout your life you have been my spokesperson of love 2,689 times. I remember everyone of them. You see, you blessed me 2,689 times. 1265 of them had children and spouses that were blessed from it as well. Of those 1265, there were 3798 children or spouses. You were not able to see the results of your giving, but I was able to demonstrate my love to 6487 people. Now, because of your obedience to me, 672 of them have already accepted our invitation to live here with us by accepting the gift of my son and the price he paid for them. I can also tell you that just over the next three generations of those families, there will be a total of 10,235 who will accept our invitation as well. You have brought me much joy."

Bill just stood there in shock! He said, "I had no idea."

God said, "You accepted my invitation through my son. Then you gave yourself to me to be used so I could express my love to others. That's all I ask."

Bill said, "It's hard to imagine that anyone would turn down your invitation to live with you in heaven."

God, replied, "You see, Bill, I created every person one at a time. I made them in my image. This means I put in them a spirit that will live forever like me--and if they would truly believe what my son had done for them, I could give them my spirit to actually live inside of them. This would give them an eternal connection with me.

"I gave them emotions just like mine to help them relate to me. I customized each of them by giving them different talents, different personalities, different skin colors, and even different fingerprints as evidence of my craftsmanship. Every one of them is beautifully and wonderfully made. They are my miracle of life. Every one of them brought joy to me as I was creating them. I also deposited in them a little faith to help them believe me when I said I loved them.

"Bill, there are two things that hurt me. The first is seeing them suffering throughout their lives. The second thing is that they don't know me. If they just knew me ,they would know how much I love them. You see, Bill, I have given all I have, and my heart just aches as I see their pain and suffering."

God said, "Well enough of me let's continue, this day is for you."

Bill looked at God with tears in his eyes and said, "Please, can we stop for a moment? I have something to say."

God said, "Sure, we never have to rush here."

Bill said, "Father, thank you for sharing your heart. You have helped me so much. I want to listen to you. I want you to be free to share yourself with me. Without it I may never get to know you as deeply as I would like.

Sue stepped in and said, "Bill, as I listened to both of you, I learned something very valuable.

Bill replied, "What's that, honey?"

"I realized that God's heart can be hurt, that he has emotions like us. This has helped me so much. I will never do anything to hurt you, my father. I love you."

They all hugged each other, and Bill said, "Now I'm satisfied. I'm free to express my love back to you. That's a beautiful thing."

Jesus said, "Well, I know that your love for us is genuine."

Sue said, "Why's that?"

Jesus replied, "Because everyone is soaking wet from the mist of the falls and no one realized it."

Bill laughed and said, "Sue calls that being off in your own world."

Sue said, "Yes, we were, and it was great!"

Both God and Jesus seemed to be very anxious as God said, "Now both of you close your eyes as we walk you in. Remember, don't open your eyes."

Bill thought, *Now I don't know why but I'm going to count each step I take. Here we go, 1..2...3………………98, 99. 100.*

Then they stopped. God said, "Keep your eyes closed for a few more seconds as we position you to receive the best view."

Bill and Sue were asked to step up onto what felt like a platform. As they did, God said, "We are in the center of this room, and we are standing on a platform that operates like an elevator. It will take us up to the top, then I will have you open your eyes. After that, it will slowly lower us as we view the layout of your cave mansion."

Bill thought, *Let's see, I took 100 steps which is approximately 100 yards to the center…...Wow! This room is the length and width of two football fields.*

They could feel the platform rising. Within a matter of seconds, they had reached the top. Then God said, "I just want to say that your lives have brought us great joy from the moment of your creation up to now. The very moment you accepted my invitation to live here with us, we started to prepare this place for you."

Bill was a little confused as he asked, "Can you tell me when and how I accepted your invitation?"

God looked at Jesus and said, "Can you tell us when Bill accepted our invitation?"

Jesus said, "Yes, I remember it well."

Jesus looked at Bill and said, "Do you remember the time you picked up a load of refrigerators and were hauling them to New York City?"

Bill thought for a moment and then responded, "Oh yeah, that was quite a trip. The traffic was terrible and the roads were icy. There were dozens of accidents, causing many delays. It turned a two day trip into a five day trip. I remember."

Jesus said, "Yep, that's the one. I remember you were so frustrated because all traffic was at a standstill. Then you turned on your radio. Can you take the story from there?"

Bill thought for a moment and replied, "Well, I remember the station I had on was a country and western station. I listened to the singer's words about how nothing was going right. His wife had thrown him out of the house, his dog was mad at him, his pickup truck wouldn't start, and someone stole his shotgun from the back window rack. The only thing he could do was to try to hitch a ride to the tavern. He began walking and no one would pick him up, so he had to walk the whole way. When he arrived and sat down at the bar, he ordered a beer. The bartender served it and said, 'That will be one dollar.' He pulled out his billfold to discover his wife took all his money, and the story keeps going on from there.

"I just had to change the channel. As I was scanning the stations, I heard Billy Graham say these words, "God is closer than a friend. He knows your every need." This sparked something inside me, so I just continued to listen as he said, 'Today everyone who hears my voice is invited to spend eternity with the one who loves you more than anything.'

I remember Dr. Graham saying that no one could ever be good enough to live in heaven because we carry with us sin. God's kingdom is without sin, so no one could ever enter. That sure grabbed my attention because I realized that there were a couple things I always wondered about. First, I tried hard to be good but I always failed. This was awful because I was never really sure if I was going to heaven or not. I remember thinking, *well I'm living a better life than most. I sure hope God takes that into consideration.* But after listening to Dr. Graham I realized that I was looking at this wrong. It wasn't about my goodness at all; it was about God's goodness--for in John 3:16, it says, 'For God so loved every person that he gave his only son as a sacrifice as payment for all their sins, and whoever believed in Jesus would have everlasting life with him.'"

Bill looked directly into Jesus' eyes. He could see the love Jesus had for him. Bill tried to hold back his emotions when he said, "Jesus, I tried hard to be good enough but I couldn't. I tried to convince myself that maybe I had a chance if I was just better than most, but that was wrong thinking also. There really was nothing I could do to make it to heaven. It was very hard for me to accept that at first, but then I realized that you were tortured, beaten, struck by whips on your bare back, with a crown of thorns placed on your head as they pushed it down so hard that the thorns would penetrate deep into your skull. As the blood flowed down your face and head from all sides, they mocked you by saying, 'Here, oh king of the Jews--here's your crown.'

"Many people laughed and celebrated your torture. After all that, you chose to carry the burden of the cross yourself, knowing that it would take you to the place of your crucifixion. There was no one there to support you, for all people had fallen short. Even your disciples ran in fear."

Bill continued to look at Jesus as tears flowed from his eyes and realized that he was looking at the very one who had died in his place. Bill looked directly into Jesus' eyes and said, "I know that the weight of the cross wasn't the only burden you carried."

Jesus replied, "Tell me what you mean by that."

Bill began to weep uncontrollably. After a period of time he was able to respond by saying, "You also carried the weight of my sin and the sin of every man, woman, and child. I'm so sorry I did that to you.

Jesus could only respond by saying, "Bill, I love you."

After Bill's emotions had subsided enough to talk he said, "When you had walked all the way to the top of the hill, you collapsed to the ground with the cross on top of you. You could hear some say, 'I hope he's not dead yet because we're not through with him.'

" Then another group of men walked over to you. It took three men to lift the cross off of you. They carried it over near a hole they had dug to set the cross in. The four men laughed as they picked you up by your legs and arms and walked near the cross that was still laying on the ground. They invited the crowd to count with them as they began swinging you back and forth while everyone counted, *one...two..three.* They released you as you flew high in the air.

"When you landed, everyone could hear the sound of the wind being forced out of your lungs. They did that in the name of fun. Then they grabbed your hands and feet and placed you on the cross. People in the background brought the spikes and sledgehammer. All mankind was completely wicked and evil.

"You were laid out on the hard, splintery wood while they drove a large spike through each hand and into the cross. Your feet were placed one on top of the other, and again a large spike was driven through both feet and into the cross.

"They raised the cross up, and everyone could hear the sounds of agony as the weight of your body pulled down on the holes in your hands. You heard them laugh as you screamed when they dropped the cross in the hole, knowing the pain you would experience when it hit bottom.

"Everyone just stood watching as you neared death. You could hear people saying in low voices, 'He's getting what he deserves.'

"Others would say, 'I never liked him, but maybe we went too far with this.'

"Some would say, 'Do you think he really is who he says he is?'

"Then there were others who just enjoyed watching you being tortured and still others who were in complete defiance as they said, 'We are finally getting rid of him, forever!'

" You slowly lost your strength, your breathing had become shallow, and the agony of death had consumed your body. With the little strength you had left, you said, 'It is finished.'

"Life rapidly left your body as your final gasp for breath failed and death came. You had paid the price for my sin, and here I stand today with you in heaven. I could never pay you back for what you have done for me."

Jesus said, "If all you had to do was be good enough to get to heaven, don't you think I would have helped you with that instead of being tortured and crucified myself? This kind of belief can only keep you out of heaven. You see, it's not about being good or being bad. Even the best people in the world have fallen short. All men have sinned.

"I tell you the truth--there is only one way to heaven, and that is to believe in me and all that I did for you. All man's sin was given to me. In God's law, forgiveness of sin could only be through blood sacrifice, not by you being a good person. My sacrifice has paid the debt for all man's sin forever. Today all my father requires from you is to believe that I did this for you. Your belief is your acceptance of my father's invitation. You see, he loves you so much that he actually made it so simple to go to heaven. Just truly believe!"

Bill was so moved by Jesus' love that he wanted to respond back with love so he said, "I don't know how to tell you how much I appreciate what you have done. What can I do to repay you?"

Jesus replied, "You have repaid me when you believed."

Bill thought to himself, *wow I never thought of it that way. He wanted me to live with him and his Father*

God so badly that they paid the debt that I had no ability to pay so I could live with them and get to know them.

"God forgive me for thinking I just had to be good enough and not valuing what you had done. Oh God, I'm so sorry."

God just looked at Bill and said, "Bill, you are here with me, and I'm so happy we can talk."

Chapter 11

ONLY GOD'S FULLNESS OF LOVE

God said, "We have had some great conversations, and my son and I have been honored by the respect you have shown and the love you have for us."

Sue thought, *WOW! I'm the one who should be saying that to him.*

Then God said, "Your obedience amazes me."

Bill replied, "What are you talking about?"

God said, "Your eyes are still closed! That's amazing."

We all laughed, and then God said, "You can open them now."

As we opened our eyes, both Sue and I were stunned at what we saw. We were lifted up to the top level of the main room. From there we could see how vast the mansion was. It was seven stories high with beautiful tunnels going from room to room.

Then we began a slow descent. We were able to see many of the rooms on each level; it was astonishing. For quite some time, the only thing Sue could say was, "I just can't believe this. Who could have ever imagined?"

Each time she said that, I would reply, " No one can imagine."

I realized that unless someone had been here, he or she would have no concept of this kind of beauty and love. They would have to experience it. There is no other way. It cannot be described. When we had descended to the ground floor, Sue and I just looked at each other for a long moment. Then I said to her, "What can I say, honey?"

Sue responded, "How could we have ever known that God loved us this much?"

I replied, "I don't think we could have. All we could have done was believe him and trust what he says is true."

Sue said, "It sure is easy now to see that everything he said in his word was true. He said, 'I love you and I'll never leave you' With all the details of our lives that he has shared with us there is no doubt that he was with us.

When Jesus said, 'I am the way, the truth, and the life, and no one can be restored back to my father except through me,' I can now see that is true. It's the price he paid for our sins that gave him the ability to invite us to live here forever. We can't be good enough. Now we are experiencing the truth of God's words when he said, 'No eyes have seen nor ears have heard of the things God has prepared for those who love him.'"

Sue continued, "Another amazing thing is God deposited a seed of faith in each of us at our creation because he knew that without faith we could never believe him."

Bill replied, "Wow, I never realized that. He has given us everything he could to make it possible for us to spend eternity with him. All we have to do is believe him."

Sue said, "That's right, and heaven is the place where he is free to show us his love. And in turn we can have the satisfaction of loving him back. WOW! That's amazing love!"

Both Bill and Sue looked over at God. Then Bill said, "You're an amazing father."

After Bill said that, Sue thought, *that's interesting, Bill called him father. Bill never knew his father; he was killed in the war when Bill was just a baby.*

Sue knew that God had touched his heart and Bill had now received the love of a father. She could tell it brought a fulfillment to him. It was like a completeness of love. *He had known the love of the mother but not the love of the father. WOW! God you are so amazing, you know everything we need.*

God said, "Well, are you ready? The best is yet to come."

Bill thought, *"that's impossible". How could it be better?*

God looked at Bill and, knowing his thoughts, he said, "Nothing is impossible for me."

Bill replied, "Yeah, you would think I'd know that by now."

God just laughed and said, "I understand, but this is how it will always be in my kingdom. I will never stop showing you the depths of my love for you."

Sue and Bill just looked at each other and said, "He is so amazing."

We stood there laughing as a flood of joy consumed us.

Chapter 12

SUE'S SPECIAL MOMENTS

A short time later, Jesus asked, "Are you ready to see more?"

Sue looked at me and asked, "Can you take more?"

I replied, "Yes, but only because of this new energetic body I've been given."

God replied, "I'm aware that your old body couldn't handle this amount of love."

Jesus said, "Let's walk through the main floor and take a closer look."

We started in the main room, which was the first room we had entered. As we began to look, I noticed that both God and Jesus had positioned themselves so we couldn't see them but they could see our reactions. The first thing that Sue noticed was a floor lamp. She walked up to it to get a closer look and said, "Oh, my God, how could you!"

I asked her, "What's going on?"

She was astonished. Then she asked, "Bill do you recognize this lamp?"

I looked closely at it and said, "Well, not really."

She said, "This was my grandmother's lamp that Mom gave me just before she died. When I was a child, I loved to spend the night at grandma and grandpa's house. This lamp was next to my bed.

"I remember after grandma would tuck me away in bed, she would pray with me, always asking God to be my closest friend. Then Grandma would kiss my forehead and say good night.

"She had grandpa put a special switch on this lamp. It was a dimmer switch that he mounted on the bed so I could reach it. Of course, I played with that every night until I fell asleep.

"When mom gave it to me after storing it in her garage for twenty years, the lamp was all dirty and tarnished and in need of repairs."

Bill said, "Yes, if I recall correctly, that was on the honey do list for quite some time."

Sue said, "God must have gotten a hold of my honey do list."

We both laughed as I thought, *wow, God even cared about her honey do list.*

I noticed God smiling. It made me feel so good as well, just watching Sue as she was being so blessed. I thought, it's *so amazing how God is able to know us so well that he gives us the very things that we cannot give to each other. It's as if he knows Sue better than I do.*

We had only taken a couple steps when something caught Sue's eye. She stopped and stared at a doll. I could see that it brought back memories. Then I noticed a tear rolling down her face, as she softly said, "This was my first doll. I was six years old. Mom and Dad bought it for me for Christmas. I remember the moment I took it in my arms. That's when it happened."

"What happened?" I asked.

Sue didn't say anything. She just reached for the doll, placed it in her arms, and pressed it tightly against her body. I watched as more tears ran down her face. Then after a few minutes she said, "I was unwrapping my Christmas present, not knowing what it was. I remember seeing a picture on the box. It was a picture of the most beautiful baby doll I had ever seen.

"I struggled trying to get the box open, so my mother helped. When she had it opened, I looked at her and said, 'Mom, can you get her out for me?'

"I watched intently as Mom pulled the doll out. Then I noticed mom's face, full of love as she held the baby doll. Then she carefully placed the doll in my arms. I immediately drew it towards my chest and gently hugged it.

"Then I remember the most beautiful feeling running through my body. For the first time, I experienced

117

a mother's love. The doll was no longer just a doll, it was a baby--my baby. I named her Sarah. I thought that was such a beautiful name. I cared for baby Sarah for a long time.

"Even after I grew up, Sarah was very special to me. Bill, when we had our first child, Diana, I felt that same mother's love when she was presented to me for the first time in the hospital. What a beautiful experience.

"I couldn't wait to get home so I could be a real mommy. I remember Diana's sixth birthday when I gave Sarah to her. When Diana reached for Sarah, she pulled her to her chest just as I had done twenty eight years earlier. As soon as Diana gave her a gentle hug, I saw it in her face--she had experienced the love of a mother. I was so blessed by that."

Bill thought, *Sue had shed many tears through her life. Almost all of them were tears of pain and suffering, but now her tears are tears of joy. I love these tears much more.* God had a way to reach down deep inside of Sue and give her this very special moment. I felt a love for God penetrating deep within me.

Chapter 13

BILL'S SPECIAL MOMENTS WITH GRANDPA

As we continued our tour, I was realizing that this mansion was more than just a beautiful place. Suddenly I started to giggle as I saw in the corner of the room a cowboy hat and cowboy boots.

I walked over, and sure enough they were my first cowboy hat and boots. I told Sue, "When I was about five years old, I would go to Grandpa's house every Friday after school. He would make some popcorn while I got two cans of pop out of the refrigerator. Grandpa always got excited having me come over to watch '*Gunsmoke*' with him."

I continued, "Grandpa would grab a huge bowl of popcorn and I would grab the pop and head to the living room. Grandpa had his special seat--you know, the brown recliner. I always thought it was our special movie seat.

"Grandpa would place the popcorn on the end table and I would do the same with the pop. Then the ritual of getting into the chair began. You see, Grandpa had a funny looking body. It didn't look like mine. He had certain parts that were too big, but that was part of what made him special.

"Only my grandpa could sit in that chair with a huge popcorn bowl on his belly, and it stayed there. It was a perfect fit. Well, Grandpa would slowly lower himself into the chair, grunting and moaning.

"I remember the first time I heard those noises, they scared me. I asked him if he was alright, and he said, 'Of course I am. I'm just talking to the chair. I'm just telling it to get ready because both of us are going to be sitting on him.'

"Grandpa talked to the chair every time we sat on him. I remember how proud I was of my grandpa because he could speak another language. I often told kids at school that my grandpa could talk chair language. No one ever believed me, but they didn't know my grandpa-- I did.

"Well, somehow I was able to stuff myself in the chair with him every time. The popcorn bowl was in the perfect place for both of us. Every week we watched *"Gunsmoke"* with Marshal Matt Dillon of Dodge City, Kansas. I always admired Marshall Dillon. I dreamed about being his deputy and going after bad guys together.

"Anyway, on my 8th birthday, Grandpa handed me an envelope. I opened it and I took out two pieces of stiff paper. I looked closer and saw in the upper left corner that it said USA Airlines. I remember I was a little disappointed as I asked Grandpa what they were.

"He said, 'These are two airline tickets to Dodge City. We are going to meet Marshal Dillon.'

I was shocked. I remember feeling both excited and nervous--excited to meet him and nervous about going after bad guys.

"Then Grandpa gave me another present. He said, 'If you're going to meet Marshal Dillon, you had better look like a cowboy.' Inside the box was a cowboy hat and a pair of cowboy boots.

"I ran up to my bedroom and put on my favorite jeans, along with a western shirt and belt that Mom bought me. Then I put on my new boots. I ran to my mirror and watched myself put on the cowboy hat. It had to be positioned just right if I was going to face the bad guys. That was the most memorable trip I had ever taken."

Sue just looked at me for a moment and said, "Well?"

I replied, "Well, what?"

She said, "You know what! Did you meet Marshall Dillon or not?"

I replied, "Of course I did! My grandpa would never lie.

"It was better than I thought. After we arrived, Grandpa watched with a big smile as I put on my new cowboy clothes. I was so proud as I looked in the mirror as I adjusted my hat until I   got the look I wanted."

Sue commented, "I guess I didn't realize you could get different looks out of it. I just thought a cowboy hat was a cowboy hat. So, honey, what look did you want to have?"

I laughed as I said, "Well, I was hoping Marshal Dillon would want me to be his deputy, so I put my hat on like this."

Bill grabbed his hat, now three sizes too small, off the wall and placed it on his head. Then Bill said, "Okay, this is the right position. Well, Sue, how does this look?"

She replied, "Well….. What look are you trying to get?"

Bill replied, "I shouldn't have to tell you. The look should speak for itself. So tell me what it says to you."

Sue thought, *I know what he wants me to say--that it makes him look like a tough and rugged cowboy, but really he looked like an overgrown kid in a little boys cowboy hat.*

After thinking about it, Sue decided to tell him. "Bill," she said as she choked back laughter, "I think it makes you look like a rough and tough cowboy."

He was off in his own little world, and Sue liked that. Then she asked him, "What happened next?"

Bill replied, "You won't believe it. Grandpa said, 'You sure do look like you would make a good deputy.'

"As we were getting ready to walk out the door, Grandpa said, 'Bill, wait a minute. I forgot to give you something.'

"Grandpa went to the closet and got a package and handed it to me. He said, 'Here--you may need this.'

"Inside was a tan cowboy vest just like the one Marshall Dillon wore. I was so excited as I ran back to the mirror to see what I looked like. *Wow,* I thought, *I look like a miniature Marshal Dillon.*

"I looked at grandpa and asked, 'Do you think Marshal Dillon looked like me when he was my age?'

"Grandpa smiled and said, 'Exactly like you.'

"I was so proud as we walked out of the room together. Grandpa drove me to a parking lot somewhere off the main road. We got out of the car, and Grandpa said, 'Follow me.'

"He was walking much faster than normal, so I asked him, 'What's the rush?'

"He replied, 'Marshal Dillon needs you right away.'

"I could feel my heart start to race as we picked up the pace even more. I stayed really close to Grandpa. I asked him, 'Why does he need me?'

"He replied, 'He needs a deputy now!'

"Finally, after what seemed to be an hour, we arrived at the Marshal's office, where Marshal Dillon was standing with two rifles, two canteens, two bed rolls, and two saddle bags.

"He looked at me and said, 'Are you Bill Thompson?'

"I said, 'Yes, sir I am.'

"Marshal Dillon said, 'Good, I'm glad you're here,' as he walked over to his horses and put all the gear on them.

"Then he said, "Bill, can I call you Billy?'

"I said, 'Fine, just don't think I'm Billy the kid, because I'm not.'

"Grandpa giggled as Marshal Dillon smiled and said, 'Come inside, Billy.'

"I walked in his office, and it looked just like it did on television. I remember thinking, *this is real, I'm really here.* Marshal Dillon walked over to his desk and took a badge out of the drawer. I couldn't believe my eyes.

"He walked over to me and said, 'Raise your right hand.' As I looked directly into his eyes he said, 'Do you solemnly swear to uphold the laws of the state of Kansas?'

"I said, 'I do.'

"Then he pinned the badge on my chest. I was in a daze; it was real, not just pretend! Then Marshal Dillon walked over to a closet, where he took out a gun belt and a six shooter.

"He said, 'Put this on. You may need it. We are going after a bad guy.'

As we were leaving, I looked over at Grandpa and said, 'Are you coming too?'

"He said, 'No, son, I'm not his deputy. I will be here when you get back.'

"Then I remember looking at him and adjusting my hat as grandpa said, 'You are a deputy U.S. Marshal and a good one at that. Now go get the bad guy.'

"I felt the confidence building in me as I mounted my horse. I was watching Marshal Dillon mounting as well. I think I did it the same way he did. As we rode off, I turned around and looked at Grandpa. I yelled, 'Thanks, Grandpa!'

"I remember tracking all day; it sure was hot. We had to camp overnight. It was just like I imagined it would be.

"Then the following morning we broke camp and started tracking again. About three hours later, we spotted the bad guy.

"Marshal Dillon yelled, 'Get off your horse! Bring your rifle and take cover!' WOW! What a rush!

"I did what he said as fast as I could. One second after I jumped behind a boulder the shooting started. The bad guy shot twice and Marshal Dillon shot back. Then there was silence, and it was over. It didn't last long enough for me to get too scared because Marshall Dillon hit him on the first shot.

"The bad guy was shot in the arm, so I helped tie him up. We got him on the horse and Marshall Dillon told me to take the rear position and keep an eye on the bad guy, and if he tried to escape just shoot him. I thought, *WOW, I'm really doing it.*

"When we arrived back in Dodge, I could see Grandpa standing in front of the marshal's office. I felt so proud of myself bringing in the bad guy. I could tell grandpa was proud of me as well. When we walked the bad guy into the office, Marshall Dillon said to me, 'Here's the keys Deputy. Lock him up.'

"I had a huge smile on my face as I threw him in jail. When I returned the keys to Marshal Dillon he thanked me by saying, 'You did a great job, Deputy. Then he handed me two meal tickets to eat at Delmonico's. I couldn't believe it. Grandpa and I were going to eat at the same restaurant Marshall Dillon ate at every week on *Gunsmoke*.

"We went to Delmonico's, and I got to share my experience with Grandpa. What a trip! Sue, I just realized that when you experienced your doll becoming your baby it's kind of like Marshal Dillon becoming real to me. That's so cool."

Chapter 14

THE UGLY PRINCESS

Everywhere we looked in this mansion we saw items that we valued more than money. They were timeless treasures of our lives. Everything was so intimate, so personal. Only God could have the capability to understand us and our lives at this incredible level.

As we continued walking, Sue began laughing. She pointed at a photograph on the wall that was taken during a family vacation. Sue said, "Look at this!"

I walked over, and as soon as I saw it I started laughing as well. Sue said, "Bill you're such a goofball."

The picture was taken in a motel room at Disney world. We had all three children with us and we had toured the park all day long. Susan, who was our youngest daughter, was so fascinated with Cinderella that she would call her a princess. Susan asked her mom if all princesses were as pretty as

Cinderella. Sue had told her they were.

On this trip, I decided to gather the whole family together along with the family dog, a ninety-pound chocolate lab, and we were all reclining on one of the queen-sized beds. I started by saying, "Let's have a family sharing time where each of us can share things about the day's activities."

Everyone was anxious to share. We all laughed at some stories and were amazed by others. We were just enjoying each other. Our dog, whose name was Coco, had a great time also. His powerful tail was wagging and hitting everyone in the face. He couldn't help it; he was excited because we were excited. His tongue was hanging out as he panted.

Then Michael, our middle child, got a big wet, dog kiss in his face. He just laughed as he wiped his face with his shirt sleeve, but the two girls were grossed out and jumped off the bed in fear of getting kissed as well.

Then I just sat still on the bed and called Coco over to me. Coco started walking on the bed awkwardly, stepping over Michael. Then he stopped in front of me, which meant he was straddling Sue. Then I asked Coco for a kiss. Coco quickly obeyed . All the kids, including Michael, were grossed out as I didn't move while receiving one wet kiss after another. The two girls got so grossed out they were screaming as they ran into the bathroom and locked the door. I told Coco to stop, figuring I had gotten all the entertainment possible out of this event. When the girls were convinced that it was over, they came out of the bathroom.

After that, we decided to continue our family sharing time. Sue said, "Yeah, we all got back on the bed, but this time us girls were laying down the rules, you would only talk about cute and pretty things."

Sue continued, "And by the way, Bill, I did notice you and Michael rolling your eyes when we said cute and pretty things. I remember thinking, *"this won't last long"*. The girls and I were talking about Cinderella and other pretty things. I noticed that you and Michael were getting very bored."

Bill said, "Yes, I remember setting the stage for what was coming. I got everyone's attention and then I said, 'Girls, are all princesses as pretty as Cinderella?'

"Susan jumped right in and said, 'Of course they are, Dad, don't you know that?'

"I replied by asking, 'Don't you think it's possible for at least one princess to be ugly?'

"Now all the girls, including Mom, were saying, 'No way, every one of them is beautiful.'

"Then I remember saying, 'I know one ugly princess.'

"The two girls didn't believe me, but Sue knew that I had something planned. The girls kept on me, insisting that I didn't know an ugly princess. I looked over at Michael and asked him to help me find her because she was here in the park.

"The two girls kept saying, 'No way, Dad, she's not here.'

"Michael and I walked out of the room. I explained to Michael that I had purchased a princess costume, and I needed him to dress up like a princess so I could present him to the girls. At first Michael was reluctant, but after a little convincing, he decided it would be fun.

I told Michael that we had to go all the way in disguising him so the girls wouldn't recognize him. He said, 'Yeah, that sounds great.'

Then he stopped and thought for a moment before asking, 'What do we have to do to make that happen?'

I opened the bag, and inside was make up, some sparkling barrettes for his hair, a pink princess dress, and a blonde wig. With each item I showed him, I could see his face becoming more and more pale.

"Let's see now..." I continued. "I've got white panty hose, and look at these pretty pink shoes. I even got you a pretty pink purse to match your pretty pink dress and your pretty pink shoes."

Michael had a sick look on his face as he asked, "Can't we get someone else to do this?"

I told him, "No, Son, because you are the perfect candidate. You are a handsome guy who would make an ugly girl."

I began to laugh, but the only response from Michael was a snort that indicated he didn't find the situation funny at all.

I told him, "Follow me, Son. We are going to have some fun."

So he followed as I took him into a bathroom near the lobby area. Once inside I started putting the makeup on. Michael was nervous, always worrying that someone was going to walk in.

Now I had never put makeup on before, and it showed. I could have taken a pretty girl and made her ugly just with a makeup job. My goal was to disguise him so well that his sisters wouldn't recognize him.

Then I put the wig on and sprinkled the shiny, glittery stuff on it. I thought, *"so far so good".* Michael kept wanting to look in the mirror, but I stopped him and told him it would be better for him to wait until we were done, so he could get the full affect.

I knew that if he saw himself then, this whole thing would be over. He really did look ugly. Then I had him put on the panty hose, and it was all I could do to keep from laughing. I think he was grossing himself out.

"Well, Michael," I said, "the dress is next." I knew this was a critical moment. I could see in his eyes that I had to say some kind of encouraging words for him to continue.

So I said, "Michael I know this is going to be a day for us all to remember. You are going to be playing the biggest trick this family has ever seen. You're making memories."

Michael responded by saying, "I'm not sure I want to remember this."

I told him, "I'm sure you will think differently later. We have come this far. Let's keep going."

Michael didn't say a word, but he slowly put the dress on. I looked at him standing there, and I wanted to say something to him but I realized that I could get in a lot of trouble here by saying things like, 'Oh, Michael you look like a princess,' or 'Michael, you look so pretty,' or 'Michael you look so ugly.' I decided to just keep my mouth shut."

Finally, I said, "Okay, just put the shoes on and grab your purse. Let's get going."

Michael gave me a dirty look and said, "Grab my purse--yeah, right."

I just responded with a nervous giggle. I didn't want him to look in the mirror because I knew this whole thing would be called off. As we started to walk to the exit door, I was thinking about telling him the role playing strategy I had, and then it happened. Just as Michael was reaching for the door handle, he suddenly stopped, looked at me and said, "There's no way.... No way am I going to walk out there dressed like this. People are going to be staring and giving me funny looks. There's no way."

I realized I had to think of something quickly or it was all over. I came up with something to say. I knew it would be risky, but I had to say something. I looked at

Michael and said, "I know this would be embarrassing if people knew who you were, but believe me when I tell you that when this is over and the makeup and costume are off, no one will even recognize you. We did a great job in disguising you."

Thankfully, that was enough to help give Michael the courage to open the door and walk out into public. I spoke softly to him as we were walking down the hallway saying, "The room is just up ahead, and there isn't anyone behind us or ahead of us. We can make it."

Michael seemed to be a little more comfortable, so I quickly told him that his princess name was Elizabeth. Then I told him to just act pretty and don't say a word. I would do all the talking. We were only a few feet from our door when Michael asked, "Dad, how do I act pretty?"

I thought for a few seconds and replied, "I don't know. Just act pretty."

Before I opened the door, I told Michael to just stand in the hallway and follow my lead. I opened the door, and the girls just stood there looking at me.

Then Diana said, 'Well, Dad, where is she? This ugly princess you said you know."

I could tell Diana wished she hadn't said that after I told her she was standing outside the door. I then announced, "I would like to present to you my friend, Princess Elizabeth."

When she walked in, I saw a shocked look on the girls' faces. They acted nervous, and they were not sure what to say.

After a few seconds Diana awkwardly said, "I'm ...pleased to meet you...you sure are a beautiful princess." Everyone in the room knew she was very ugly, so this just added to the awkwardness.

I noticed that Sue was staring very intently at the princess. I could see by her expression that she had just figured out that it was Michael.

I thought, *I hope she plays along with us for a while.* Then Susan, who was only five years old and the princess expert in the family, walked up to the princess and started examining her. Susan was never much for keeping her thoughts to herself, and I didn't expect that she would be any different now.

She asked the princess for her hand, felt it and announced, "Your hands are not princess soft." I remember thinking, *I didn't even know there was such a thing as princess soft.*

She said, "You didn't paint your fingernails. Princesses always paint their fingernails."

I could see that Michael was getting a little nervous, but he was still maintaining the role. Then Susan began sniffing the air and said, "You're not wearing princess perfume. I have some of that, you know."

Then she saw the silver sparkles in her hair and said, "Princesses do have sparkles in their hair, but they are gold sparkles."

I wondered how she knew that. When Susan asked the princess who her prince was, Michael just looked at me waiting for my response. I thought to myself, *there is a lot about this princess stuff that I don't know.*

I just looked at her and said, "The princess can't talk right now. She has an important speaking engagement tonight, so she is saving her voice."

Susan gave me a funny look and said, "You can't fool me, Dad. I know a princess when I see one, and this isn't one."

The whole thing backfired on me. I had been "busted" by a five-year-old princess expert. Suddenly, there was a flash from a camera. Sue got the perfect picture of the look on my face when I realized the trick was on me. How could I have thought that I knew enough about the topic to fool them?

Susan walked up to me, and stood there looking up at me. I remember thinking how tiny she looked. Then, in her little tiny girl voice, she said, "Dad, I knew it was Michael as soon as he came in. You need to make sure you know about princesses before you try something like that again."

I replied, "You're right, and if I need an expert on princesses I will make sure to call you."

Susan just smiled and walked across the room where she picked up her princess doll and began to play. I learned a lesson that day. Don't ever try to trick any female--big or small-- by using the male brain only, especially in areas where the ladies are experts. They really do know their stuff.

Sue and I both laughed as we finished reliving the memory together.

Chapter 15

FOREVER DISCOVERING

Sue and Bill had spent about six hours just enjoying the main room, and there was much more to see. We realized that the mansion could take a lifetime to tour because it was filled with great memories. Sue remarked that she thought it sounded crazy but she was starting to actually enjoy her past years even more after seeing the mansion.

Bill replied, "I agree. We had a better life than what we realized."

Sue said, "Yes, Bill, I'm starting to see that now."

Sue looked at God and asked, "Father, would it be correct to say that this mansion is so large that it would take us a whole lifetime to tour?"

God replied, "It will take much longer than that."

Sue was surprised by his answer. She looked at Bill as she had a quick revelation. She said, "Bill, this is going to be like the home decor programs I watch. You see how surprised people are when they open their eyes to see their beautiful newly decorated house?"

Bill said, "Okay..." as he thought, *I'm not sure I get the connection.* Then he said, "I'm not sure what you mean. Tell me more."

Sue was excited and said, "Think about this. Every day we get up and tour our house. We never see the same thing twice, and it's like that forever."

She continued, "God must know us girls well. It's like he has given me my own decor discovery show."

Bill thought for a moment, then he turned toward God and asked, "Father, how big is this mansion?"

He replied, "As big   as you want it to be."

Bill looked at God in confusion and said, "I know for sure I can't wrap my brain around that one."

God replied, "And if you do you will only make your mansion smaller."

I looked at God and said, "Are you just playing mind games with us?"

God said, "I understand, because I know where you came from, but realize that in my kingdom you never have to figure anything out. There is no benefit in it. Actually it holds you back. This may help you understand. In my kingdom you will always be searching, as you are now. You will discover many things. In everything you discover, you will see me. My love, my beauty, my understanding, my mercies, and many things you never realized before.

"In the short period of time that you have been with me, you've only had a taste of what it will be like continually and forever! You are already fascinated by what you have discovered, and this is what will keep you searching for my discoveries. The more you discover, the more you know me. The more you know me, the more you love me. You cannot imagine where that leads to over time."

All Bill could say was WOW and thank you!

Sue said, "WOW is right. Can I have friends to share this with?"

Jesus replied, "All you could ever want. Every good thing is in abundance here."

Bill said, "Okay, just one last question."

God said, "Okay, but there is no rush. Ask all the questions you want."

Bill observed, "There are seven stories of rooms here, but I don't see any stairs or the elevator we took earlier. So how do I get up there?"

Sue giggled as she asked God if she could answer that.

God said, "Sure, go ahead."

"Do you remember how we got from God's mansion to here?"

Bill replied, "Yes, how could I forget that?"

Sue said, "Well, that's how everyone travels here. You just desire to be somewhere, and you are there."

Sue looked at God and asked, "Is that correct?"

God said, "Yes, that's right."

Bill said, "Well, God, now that I know that, I'm wondering why I had to take an elevator up to the top level when we first arrived."

God replied, "Bill look over there," as he pointed to where the elevator platform was located.

As they looked Bill said, "God, the platform isn't there."

God said, "That's right and you will never need one again. I wanted to take you to the top where you could experience the beauty of this place. I wanted you to enjoy the full impact of that moment. I knew that if we all just ascended there, you wouldn't be able to have the fullness of the beauty because you would have been trying to figure out how you got up there."

Bill replied, "God, you don't want any distractions to block the blessings you have for us, do you?"

God replied, "I think they have been blocked from all people for way too many years. That will never happen to you here."

Bill and Sue fell to their knees and worshipped them and thanked them for everything they had done. Because of what they had experienced, they realized that throughout their whole lives, they could only receive a very small portion of joy and love that comes with God's blessings. It was as if they had been too bound up to receive the full benefit of them.

Jesus asked if we were ready to go back outside so they could explain some things about their kingdom. Sue replied, "Yes, that would be great. There's no rush to tour something that you will be touring for eternity."

Bill just shook his head and said to Sue, "Could you have ever believed just two days ago that you could make a statement like that?"

Sue thought for a moment and replied, "No, I couldn't even imagine that, but the beautiful thing is that I'm already becoming comfortable in saying such things. All my life I thought about what this could be like. I remember talking with friends about heaven.

"The only thing we could do is ask each other, but we never really got answers. We all knew it was going to be good. We all knew it was a place where we worshipped God.

"I remember a time in our conversations about heaven when one of my friends said, 'Well, I guess I will just put on my angel outfit and get on my knees and worship for eternity.' She added, 'That doesn't sound like the place I want to go forever.'

Another friend said, 'Well, I've been married to my husband for thirty-nine years, and I don't want to die and never have him again. I want him forever.'

"These are just a few of many misconceptions people have about heaven," God replied. "With what you have experienced here, can you tell me what you have learned so far?"

Sue replied, "Father, there has been so much going on the last day and a half that I could speak of your love forever."

Bill stepped in and said, "That almost says it all."

He looked at God and said, "You are love. We can only know the fullness of your love in living here with you. Heaven is your kingdom of love."

Sue said, "Yes God, it's your kingdom, and it is a place where true and pure love is received and expressed."

Bill said, "God, because I now understand how much you love and value our lives, I just wish everyone would know you, not just about you."

God had a tear rolling down his face, and Bill reached in his back pocket and pulled out a silk handkerchief to wipe it away.

Then Bill said, "I know it breaks your heart, and it now it breaks mine, too."

Chapter 16

GIVE AND IT WILL BE GIVEN UNTO YOU

The group walked out the mansion's entrance and passed by the waterfalls. Then they stopped and looked at all the spacious and beautiful land. Jesus said, "Bill, you and Sue both said you had green thumbs."

They looked at each other and nodded their heads in agreement. Jesus said, "This gift was given to you by my father. It is to be used here as a blessing to others that live here, which includes people as well as animals. You see, this is what you give, while others will have different gifts to give. Now, in my father's kingdom there is always abundance."

Jesus pointed toward an apple tree where a whitetail deer was approaching. Jesus said, "Now watch closely what happens." The deer pulled an apple off and started eating it. Instantly, another apple replaced it.

Jesus said, "Now would you go and pick the new apple and bring it back?"

Bill walked up to the tree. He didn't say anything, but he noticed the deer was not scared of him. He picked the apple and walked back. Jesus said, "Now hand it to me."

He continued, "Now, Sue, I want you to take a bite of the apple and hand it to Bill, and he will take a bite as well."

Sue, who knew the Bible quite well, said, "Are you sure, Jesus? This sounds like Adam and Eve all over again."

Jesus said, "I assure you that will never happen again."

Sue took a bite, and then Bill, and Jesus asked them how it tasted.

"Delicious," they replied.

Jesus said, "Everything here is replaced immediately, fully ripened and ready to eat. There is an everlasting abundance, so be free to give to all who ask. You give, and it will be given also to you, when you ask. You will ask for only what you need, but you will always receive more than you ask for. That's how it is in my father's kingdom. You will learn in time that it's better to give than to receive."

God began to share more about how the economy of heaven works. He said, "As my son has told you, the gift that I gave you at creation is a gift that you will use forever in my kingdom. There are many that live in my kingdom who have different gifts. In my kingdom, if you have a need, you just ask the one with that gift, and you will receive what you ask for and more. There is no charge for anything here. We ask when we need, and we give when asked. You will never lack in anything.

"In my kingdom, we are interdependent not independent. Independence will lead you to poverty. Hoarding or holding back will lead to poverty. I understand that this is so different from where you came from, but here you will quickly learn what I am telling you.

"Everyone here is already aware of your arrival and the location of this place I have prepared for you. You will see that when you have a need, you only need to ask and your need will be met. That's really all there is to it. There are no banks, insurance companies, cars, gasoline stations, doctors, hospitals, police, jails, taxes, heat bills, electric bills, house payments, food costs, pharmacies, drugs, violence, death, or punching the time clock. There is no deterioration of any kind, no landscape needed, no lawn care, no bills, and no money. All I ask is that you enjoy the gifts I've given you, be generous to others, enjoy your life, and love me and other people.

"Oh, a few more things, that we don't have here are disappointments, pain or suffering of any kind and no sin. Also, Sue, I know you have one more question. Can you ask me now?"

Sue answered, "Yes, my father. I noticed when Bill went to get the apple off the tree that the deer was not scared of him. Why?"

God answered, "One of the curses of the first sin was that animals would fear man. In my kingdom, there is no sin. As a result, animals do not fear man, nor do they fear each other. They are here for your enjoyment only. You can call any animal to you, and it will come. You can freely pet them and enjoy their love and beauty."

Sue always loved animals and nature shows. She said, "God you are so good. You bring a fullness in all life."

Bill began to look closely at every tree and every plant. They were so healthy and full of life. Not one blade of grass or a flower was dead. Nothing showed any signs of sickness or aging.

Bill laughed as he said, "And no worms in the apples, that's awesome."

God said, "You are correct. There is no sickness or disease of any kind in my kingdom. Everything lives forever. As you are discovering, my kingdom is very different than what you have been used to.

"You see, when people first come here they often struggle because they can't figure out how to get something they need. Always remember this--you don't have to figure out anything in my kingdom. All you have to do is ask and you will be given more than you asked for. You will have abundance in all you ask for. It's just that simple.

" Bill, I was proud of you earlier. When I was weeping and a tear run down my face, you wanted to wipe my tear, so you reached inside your pocket for a handkerchief and--voila--it was there.

Bill thought for a moment and said, "I desired to wipe your tear so I reached in the place I thought it would be and--voila--it's there."

God said, "That's what I meant when I said I would give you the desires of your heart."

Everything became quiet as the four of us stood looking at each other. Normally this would be one of those awkward moments when no one had anything to say, but it didn't feel awkward. Bill looked into God's eyes and saw his love, a love that only he could have. Every time Bill looked at him, he could feel God's love and acceptance. He was comfortable to just be himself, and that felt good. It sure wasn't like this where he lived before.

Chapter 17

ONE LAST THING FOR YOU

God looked at Jesus and said, "Isn't there one more place we need to show them today?"

Jesus replied, "Yes, we probably need to do that now, because I'm not sure I can keep them from busting out much longer."

Sue got all excited and asked, "What kind of animals did you get for us? You know I love little fluffy kittens."

Bill said, "Sue, I really can't see Jesus having a problem keeping little kittens in their cages. If it's kittens, then it's probably a lion or a tiger or something like that."

That made Sue even more excited, and she said, "That's so beautiful. I'm just going to hug them and kiss them, and pet them, and tell them how much I love them."

Bill said, "Well, God, your kingdom is love all right, and by the looks of things she will be spending her time loving the animals, the flowers, the neighbors, the beautiful mansion, the beautiful landscape, and whatever else you could think of. There will be a lot of lovin' going on around here. I just hope there's time for me to be on that lovin' list as well."

Jesus said, "Since time is not an issue here, I'm sure she will fit you in."

We all laughed as Jesus escorted us back to our mansion. Jesus stopped as we approached the waterfalls. He looked at us and said, "Love always wants to share life with others."

Sue said, "That's right."

Then Jesus said, "Both of you stand face to face and look directly into each other's eyes."

We stood there for several minutes. Bill thought, *this is amazing--the longer I look at her, the deeper I see in her.* I realized there was one element of pain left in her. I wasn't sure what it was, but I just continued to look deeper. Then I saw a part of her heart that was quietly grieving. I realized with everything that has happened in the last two days it would have been easy for me to not see this.

Suddenly, I saw a tear roll down Sue's cheek. Then one rolled down mine. I begin to grieve with her. Now I knew what it was. God said, "Bill, do you see why her heart is grieving?"

Bill replied, "Yes, I do, Father."

"What can you do to help her?" Bill didn't say a word; he just continued looking into her eyes. Bill thought, *in the past there were times when I knew Sue was hurting. Sometimes I knew why and sometimes she just buried it deep within her and I didn't know why.*

In the past, Sue was the spiritual leader of my family. I liked it that way. Down deep I knew it was my responsibility, but I didn't want to step into that position because I didn't want to fail. I always justified it by telling her, "I've got enough load to carry around here. I'm taking care of the food and clothing and shelter--you know, all the important things. The least you can do is take care of the little things like the kids" and that included their spiritual lives.

I'd always end by saying, "Come on, honey, we are a team, aren't we?"

This worked every time. I knew that if we failed spiritually, I could just put the blame on her. Now I could see that I was a coward. Instead of me stepping onto the front lines of this battle, I had put her out there to fight my battles for me. No wonder she was always hurt and wounded. I put her out there to be slaughtered!

I saw what a terrible thing I had done, and I fell to my knees as the agony consumed my whole body. My heart was torn apart. How could I have done this to her? I love her so very much. I was still on my knees as I continued to weep for a long period of time. Then I felt a hand resting on each of my shoulders.

I opened my eyes and I saw Sue facing me on her knees. Just as I was going to tell her how sorry I was, she touched my lips with her finger. I just looked in her eyes; they were the eyes of mercy. She placed the palms of her hands gently on my cheeks. Then I could feel the pressure of her fingers as she held my cheeks firmly. I knew that she wanted me to listen closely to what she was going to say. Her eyes were penetrating deep inside me. She said, "Bill, I forgive you."

Instantly, I felt a wave of mercy run through me. It completely washed away every regret, every bit of my guilt and condemnation. I felt clean and free. We both stood up and reached out to each other. As we stepped forward, we came together and embraced. We pressed our bodies tightly against each other, as if we couldn't get close enough. This embrace communicated our desire to go deeper in our love relationship. It was a beautiful experience. Both of us had been healed of our wounds, and now we were free to love one another. What an amazing love!

I knew we had become closer than ever. Sue was filled with joy. I could see that this was something she had longed for for many years. She just wanted to be free to love her man. Sue said, "Bill, I'm so thankful because your repentance has helped me to be set me free to love you again."

Bill looked at God and said, "Because of your forgiveness for us, we are able to forgive each other. Just being with you heals every hurt and wound we have in us. You're a wonderful father. Thank you for forgiving us."

God said, "It's because I love you."

Then God said to Jesus, "Have they broken out yet?"

Jesus replied, "Not yet, but I don't think I can hold them back for more than a few seconds."

Sue got excited; she thought it could never get any better than this. Then God asked them to stand outside, face the waterfalls, and close their eyes. Bill thought, *well here we go again with another great view.*

God said, "There is only one more thing that I want to show you today. In my kingdom there is no lack of joy, only fullness of joy. I've done a great work in you so you will forever receive the fullness of joy in all your present and future blessings. There are three things that both of you lack before your joy can be complete. In my kingdom there is no lack, so I am honored to present to you your fullness of joy--Diana, Michael and Susan. Open your eyes!"

What happened next could only be described as an explosion of joy! Bill and Sue ran toward their children with their arms reached out. This was a moment they had always hoped would happen. The children, who were now adults, ran towards their mom and dad like young children who had been lost in the woods. When they came together, it was a family hug--all five being hugged at the same time. Not a word was spoken for several minutes as they shared smiles and expressions of love, amazement, and joy. It was a family reunion they would never forget. The family's close connection was obvious; it was a connection that was different than most. It was a union that could not be divided. There was no independence to be found. Their lives were obviously connected for the purpose of one mission. God thought, *soon they will understand the significance of the family hug.*

Both God and Jesus delighted in the family's reunion. When the time was right, God and Jesus joined them in the celebration. Bill said, "Okay, everybody, we are going to do a big family hug again--only this time it will be with God and Jesus included."

God thought, *Bill will soon understand the significance of his desire to do this.* As they came together in a group hug, each one was imparted with a bond that couldn't be broken.

God and Jesus bade them farewell and said, "Continue to enjoy each other and everything I have given you. You are a great blessing to me. When you want to be with me,, just ask and I will be with you." The whole family gave thanks and stood there watching them as they walked out of sight.

Then Michael observed, "Wow, what an amazing love."

Chapter 18

WE'VE GOT WHAT WE ALWAYS WANTED

Sue said, "Well, Diana and Susan, I think we should prepare a feast for these guys. Our first family feast in our new home. They were excited about that, so Sue said, ask and you shall receive and I ask that we go to the kitchen and--voila…. They began to prepare a feast fit for a king."

Bill looked at Michael and said, "You know a lot more about this place than I do. You've been here for a little over twenty eight years now."

Michael said, "Yeah, I suppose so, but I really don't know because we don't have calendars here. Time is not something we think about. There are no schedules or appointments here. When you need to meet someone or do something, you just know when it's time."

Bill said, "It may take me a while to figure that one out." Bill paused as he thought for a moment, then said, "No, I want to rephrase that. It may take me time to get used to that. I don't try to figure anything out around here anymore. I know firsthand that it's impossible to wrap your brain around anything. God's ways are not known by man. I've learned that discovering God is what this life with him is all about. Always going from one beautiful discovery to another."

Michael replied, "You are absolutely correct. I know thousands of people who have lived here for probably thousands of years and they are just as amazed as you and me. Dad, in as few words as possible I will tell you what these discoveries are."

Michael paused momentarily as tears began to fill his eyes. "First, I must say that my emotions come from two different things--I've seen God's heart and his deep, deep love for me, and I've also seen his grieving heart for those who don't know of his love for them. You see, Dad, my love for him is great, and the more I discover who he is the deeper love I have for him. God is one hundred percent love. A true and pure love. He is perfect love. It is this kind of love that causes everyone here to keep moving forward in their discoveries. His love draws us closer to him, and in turn our love for him grows deeper. It's amazing, Dad. It's amazing love."

Bill thought for a moment, then said, "As amazing as it's been for your mom and I in just the last thirty seven hours, I can see we have only gotten a small taste of God's love and goodness. As I stand here, I'm amazed at the indescribable love your mom and I have been shown, and to think that this is just a small taste of it. I agree it's an amazing love. What else can I say?"

Michael responded, "There is no other way to describe it. It's beyond words and, sadly, it's beyond belief by many."

When Michael said that, Bill felt a sadness inside him for those who didn't know that God loved them. Bill just quietly said, "God's love has to get through to them."

Michael said, "Well, Dad, it's that time."

Bill looked at him for a moment then remembered, "Oh, yeah, it's supper time."

Michael giggled and said, "You're catching on, Dad."

Bill laughed as he said, "Time to eat will probably be the easiest thing for us guys to catch on to."

Michael said, "Okay, Dad, what do you think the second easiest thing will be?"

Bill said, "That's easy--just say dining room please, and--voila... Here we are."

Bill saw a beautiful display of food and candle-lit atmosphere with expensive table setting and huge bowls of every kind of fresh fruit and berries. There were beautiful flower arrangements. All the girls were wearing silk apron and having the time of their lives preparing this feast. Obviously, they got everything they asked for."

In that moment, Bill realized that God wanted to make sure they would receive the full blessing as they served us. As he watched them serving, Bill was blessed by their joy. Then it happened! He burst out in laughter as he saw the centerpiece. He was laughing so hard that everyone else couldn't help but to laugh too. He slapped his knees several times, and then he would stand straight up and seal his lips tightly as he attempted to get himself under control. That didn't work; he'd just break out laughing again. The laughter had increased to the level that our whole family was rolling on the floor uncontrollably.

Finally, Bill was able to get a few words out and he asked, "What are you guys laughing about?"

Diana barely got the words out and said, "I don't know."

Well that just caused everyone to laugh all the more.

Bill thought to himself, *well at least I know what I'm laughing about.* After what seemed to be an hour or so, they got off the floor and gained most of their composure back. Sue looked at Bill and said, "I know what you're laughing about, but the kid's don't."

Bill said, "You do? What is it?"

Sue, pointed at the roasted pig with an apple in his mouth in the center of the table.

Bill said, "You're right." Then Bill and Sue began laughing while the three kids just looked at each other and shrugged their shoulders.

"Do any of you get it?" Michael asked. The girls just shook their heads no. They just watched as their mom and dad enjoyed their inside joke.

Susan asked, "Now are you going to let us in on your inside joke?"

Diana said, "Go ahead, Dad, explain it a little more."

Bill said, "Your mom and I were walking down the hallway in God's mansion. We were going to be the guests of honor for a dinner with the king of Godsville and his son. I told your mom that I had it all figured out what this dinner would be like. You know, all the servants and a huge feast sitting at their $250,000.00 banquet table. Do you get the picture?"

Diana replied, "Yeah, I think so. You had it all figured out, right?"

Sue was standing there with the smirk on her face, then she said, "Bill do you have anything more to tell us?"

He said, "Okay, okay, I told your mom they would have a roasted hog with an apple in its mouth, and of course I was wrong."

They all laughed, and Bill decided to join them and laugh at himself as well. Then Bill said, "Okay, everyone, just understand that at that time I didn't know too much about how things worked around here."

Sue just giggled as she said, "Bill, that was only yesterday."

As they were all finding their seats at the table Michael said, "I need your attention, everyone. I want to say something to Dad that I know each of you would agree to."

Michael grabbed Bill's arm as he guided him to the seat at the head of the table. He pulled out the chair and asked Bill to sit. When Bill sat down, he realized that something had just changed on the inside of him. Then Michael said, "On behalf of all of us here, we would like to show our respect for you and ask that you always sit in this seat of honor in our family."

Bill received those words from Michael and in a few seconds was transformed into the spiritual leader of his family. Bill knew that he would never again leave the spiritual leadership of his family to Sue. Bill suddenly realized that when the family took their seats at the table they were actually taking their position in the family. That every seat had it's place and purpose. For the first time, his family was in it's right position. The whole family stood up and cheered and clapped as Bill sat, amazed.

As he smiled he looked at each of them, his love and respect for them grew stronger. He knew they were a family that God had blessed. He knew he was in the seat of honor, but he sensed it would become the seat of a general.

When the family sat down Bill stood up and said, "You have shown me your respect and honor, and for that I thank you and God, who has allowed me to experience what he has always wanted for all husbands and fathers-- respect. Now, because we have accepted God's invitation to live with him, we have discovered who God is and the love he has for us. As a result of His love, we have discovered our perfect lives, our perfect family, and our perfect world. For that we all can thank our two closest friends, God and Jesus!"

The whole family stood up and began to worship God and give thanks. As they began eating, Bill watched Sue looking content at her surroundings--the beautiful home, the beautiful atmosphere with no stress, no pain, no problems, and a beautiful family just loving and enjoying each other as they feasted on the delicious food that she and her daughters had prepared. At last, she had found her perfect place, and that meant so much to me.

When the celebration had ended, Bill said, "This has been the most unbelievable family experience we have ever had, so I want this memory to be forever etched in our minds. Would you all agree?"

Susan said, "Of course we would, Dad, but why would it not be?"

Bill replied, "We can't leave this big mess for your mom to clean up. So, I've decided to do something to help."

No one said a word. They just looked at him as he said, "Well, Sue, you have cleaned up way too many of our messes over the years, so tonight I see we have a very big mess. I figure it about time I help by cleaning up this mess. I will clean it up all by myself, so you all can just go to bed now."

Everyone just stood there thinking, *he still hasn't figured this place out.* Then Bill said, "I would like for this mess to be taken care of, so just get out of my way so I can get started." As he expressed his desire.........voila--it was cleaned up.

Bill acted a little surprised, so Sue asked, "Honey, did you know what you were doing when you expressed your desire, or was it done by accident?"

Bill proclaimed, "Of course I knew what I was doing."

No one in the family was convinced that was the case, but they decided to let it rest and go to bed.

Chapter 19

ALL I HAVE TO GIVE, I GIVE TO YOU

The next morning Sue and I woke up at the same time. I could sense that something had changed since last night's celebration. This morning I didn't feel like talking. Something was going on inside of me.

As Sue was getting out of bed she said, "Good morning, honey."

"Good morning to you," I replied. That was all that was said. I thought, wow, this was sure different than yesterday morning. I could tell something was different about her as well. I just wanted to spend some time alone.

Sue went in the bathroom and showered and got dressed. When she came out she said, "Bill, I'm sorry for not being talkative this morning, but I just need to spent a little time alone to process some of the feelings I'm having right now. I'll be in the kitchen preparing breakfast. Would you please give me a half hour or so by myself?"

I replied, "Okay, honey, I need to do the same myself. I'm sure this will all work out fine."

I had a fairly good idea what was brewing inside of me, but I needed a better understanding. Now that I was all alone, I began to pray and ask God to help me understand what was going on and to guide us through this process. I was surprised because he didn't show or tell me anything. I thought, *well that's weird.*

A short time later, I went to the kitchen where Sue and the two girls were preparing a fantastic meal. I did notice that the girls were quiet as well. Then I heard someone walk into the kitchen. I turned and saw that it was Michael. He didn't say anything but appeared to be in deep thought.

This whole thing was weird. I thought, *was there something in the food we ate or what?* Then I just stopped and said to myself, *come on now, you know no one is sick and it's not about food.* The girls quietly put the food on the table as we all took   our seats.

I looked at everyone; their heads were lowered and their eyes were looking down. I knew that it would be easy for me to do that as well, but I am the leader of this family so right then I decided I was going to lead them out of this.

I began by asking in a soft voice, "Can I share with you what's going on inside of me right now?"

They all wanted to hear, so I began. "Well, last night I tossed and turned. I doubt that I got more than two hours sleep. Did any of you experience the same thing?"

All of them acknowledged that they had. "Well, I want to say that last night I had the same dream over and over. In the dream I found myself in a tough situation, but I'm not quite sure what the situation was. I do know that each dream started with my desire to give a gift back to God for everything he has done for us."

Michael spoke out and said, "I had that dream too!"

Sue and the girls acknowledged the dream also. "Well, with that said, let's start by discussing some possible gifts we could give them."

Each were able to share their ideas. Sue said, "How about a delicious fruit and berry box?"

Michael said, "Well, how about I give some of the handmade furniture I made?"

Susan said, "That's great. How about I make a blanket with our family portrait on it?"

Diana said, "I like that idea. I can add on to that by making a golden robe for each of them."

Everyone agreed that would be good. Then everyone just sat there and looked at each other. There was a complete silence in the room.

I knew what each of them were being faced with a very tough situation, and it would take a tremendous amount of courage to speak out. The silence went on for nearly a half an hour. As every minute went by we could feel the pressure increasing to say it. It was a heart wrenching decision that had to be made. Finally, I said, "Does anyone have anything to say?"

Everyone just lowered their heads in response. I thought for a moment. I realized that the statements I was going to make were risky in more than one way. I knew I was the leader of this family, so I moved the process forward by saying, "While all your suggestions are nice, I'm just not satisfied with that. There has to be something more we can give."

I struggled with what to say next. On one hand I knew what I was to do, yet on the other side I knew that if they didn't see things the way I did it could result in our family breaking up. I was particularly concerned for Sue. There was still silence in the room when suddenly Sue stood up.

All eyes were on her and everyone was intently listening to her as she said, "I think we need to go back."

There was a pause for several seconds, and then, like an explosion, joy filled the room. The whole family was cheering and celebrating as they gave thanks to God.

In the atmosphere, there was excitement for what was to come.

After the celebration subsided, I stood up and said, "By the looks of things, am I correct in saying that each of us have decided to go back? I believe we are all in agreement in the decision to go back. Is that correct?" Everyone acknowledged their agreement.

I looked at Michael and asked, "Why are you doing this?"

"Well, Dad," he replied, "because I love God and I know this would bring him his fullness of joy."

Then Diana said, "It will also bring the fullness of joy back to us as well."

Sue said, "I'm so proud of you kids!"

"So am I," I agreed. "Honey, we have found everything we ever desired and more when we found this place. Are you sure you are willing to give it all up to go back to the world of oppression?"

She replied, " If I didn't I could never be satisfied."

Susan said. "Well, what are we waiting for? Let's go talk to them."

I looked at my family with tears in my eyes. They had come to know God and his love so well that they were willing to give such a huge sacrifice as this. Their decision was by their own free will. They knew God would love them just the same if they had decided differently. What an amazing love!

We met with God and Jesus at their mansion. They greeted us and invited us in. Sue and I were amazed at the mansion's beauty, even though we had seen it the day before yesterday.

Sue remarked, "God, your mansion looks different then when we were here two days ago."

God replied, "Sue, you've known that my mercies are new every morning, but you didn't know that my decor is new every morning."

She looked at Jesus and said, "I believe him, but that's hard to believe."

Jesus said, "Sue think carefully to what I'm going to share with you. My father couldn't lie if he wanted to. You see, he is God and everything he speaks has to happen. My father is very careful with his words because of that. So everything he says is true."

Sue softly said to herself, "He's so amazing. Living here in heaven with him is an amazing journey of discoveries about who he is."

She thought, "I'll certainly miss this place."

Bill said, "Father, can we all sit down where we can talk?"

Jesus invited them into a beautiful sitting room. God opened by saying, "I'm so glad to see you all together. Tell me what's on your mind."

Bill leaned forward in his chair. God knew Bill wanted to have a serious talk, so he also leaned forward and gave him his full attention. Bill started by saying that they celebrated last evening and it was the greatest family time that any of them had ever had. Then Bill said, "This morning when we were all eating breakfast, we decided that as a family we were going to give a gift back to you."

He continued, "So each of us decided to give to you something from the gifts you had given us when you created us. Sue and I were going to give you a huge basket of fruit and berries. All the kids were going to make very nice gifts as well. While we were listening to what each had to contribute, it sounded like it would be a great combination of gifts. After each one shared, we all just sat there saying nothing. It was as if our 'nice gifts' just weren't good enough. None of us were satisfied with that. A while later, Sue stood up and stated, 'We need to go back.' That statement pierced each of our hearts. We were faced with a very tough situation."

God said, "I understand what you are saying."

Then Sue said, "Father, today I stand in a place that I have longed for all my life. I couldn't have imagined that your love for me was this incredible. I now have it all--the perfect life, the perfect family, in the perfect world. I couldn't have asked for more. I can leave that behind, but what I can't leave behind is you."

Tears began to fill her eyes as God walked up to her, wrapped his loving arms around her, and said, " Sue, I will never leave you. I will be with you wherever you go. I will put in you and your family my spirit as tangible evidence of my commitment to you. It is through my Holy Spirit that I will talk with you and walk with you. I will be closer to you than a friend."

God then addressed the whole family with tears in his eyes as he said, "Today every one of you has given to me the greatest gift possible. Your gift is given as an expression of your love for me, the highest form of expression possible by man. It's the gift I value the most-- and that gift is your life. So I am honored to accept each of your gifts."

Bill said to God, "Now, concerning my wife's statement of going back, I would like to ask on behalf of my family that we may be permitted to go back to where we came from, in order that we may speak of your love to those who don't know your love."

God paused for a moment as the tears rolled down his face. Bill and his family realized that God and Jesus were receiving the love that the family had just given them. This was a beautiful moment, and they were not going to rush it. Sue and Bill had enjoyed many such moments while in Heaven. The love they had received was one sided, but now they were giving love back to God and it brought the fullness of joy!

The longer the father and son sat there receiving our love, the more joy we received. That was so satisfying, such a completed love for everyone. At that moment we realized that it was better to give love than to receive love.

Some time later God looked at all of us and said, "No greater love has a man than to lay down his life for another. That is what you all have done. Just like my son, Jesus, you chose to give up your perfect lives, your perfect family, and your perfect world to go back to the world of sin and oppression.

"Like my son, Jesus, you know the sacrifice ahead of you, all the pain and suffering that will be inflicted upon you. Like my son, Jesus, you loved me enough to see my agony as I watch my people suffer on the earth. Like my son, Jesus, you shared in my burden of love for all people who don't know me. Like my son, Jesus, you realized the greatest gift you could ever give me is your life. You have made my love complete. I am eternally grateful!"

Again tears rolled down his face. I knew I had given him the gift he valued the most, and that was me. I thought, *what an amazing love.* I began to weep as I realized how valuable every life was to him, and all along I had never believed that I had any value to him. The reality is, it didn't matter how messed up I was. He valued me enough that while I was still a sinner He allowed his only son Jesus to give up his life to save mine. What an amazing love! I thought, *how could anyone not want that?*

Then everyone's emotions subsided and God said, "I am honored to grant your request." Our whole family began clapping their hands and danced in celebration. It was another beautiful experience as I watched my wife and children so loved by God and so much in love with Him.

God said, "Okay, everyone, I want your full attention! Now that I have honored your request, I am fully aware of the sacrifices you will make. I want you to leave here with these five promises. Number one--everything I have given you will be here when you return. Promise number two--there will be another awards ceremony upon your return, but this time it will be honoring your whole family. It will be greater than the first. Promise number three--always remember, I will never leave you or forsake you. Promise number four--you and your family will never be separated again. Promise number five--I will place in you my Holy Spirit. I have written them on each of your hearts. Now go with these promises."

As we turned to leave Jesus said, "Bill, stop. I have something for you. It's something you will need where you're going."

Jesus handed me a small box. I opened it, and inside was my dad's Rolex watch that Mom gave me for my wedding present. I had lost it on my honeymoon night. I looked at Jesus and said, "Thank you so very much. I've always felt bad about losing that."

As I was putting it on, I noticed the time. It was exactly 9am. I turned and whispered to Sue, "Exactly 48 hours in heaven!"